D0053540

SARAH'S FLAG
FOR
TEXAS

Jane
Alexander
Knapik

Illustrated by
J. Kay Wilson

EAKIN PRESS ★ Austin, Texas

FIRST EDITION

Copyright © 1993
By Jane Alexander Knapik

Published in the United States of America
By Eakin Press
A division of Sunbelt Media, Inc.
P.O. Drawer 90159, Austin, TX 78709-0159

ISBN 0-89015-900-9

Library of Congress Cataloging-in-Publication Data

Knapik, Jane.
    Sarah's flag for Texas / by Jane Alexander Knapik : illustrated
by J. Kay Wilson
        p. cm.
    Summary: Living in Texas in the 1830s, twenty-three-year-old
Sarah sees many significant changes as the area moves to
declare its independence from Mexico.
    ISBN 0-89015-900-9 : $12.95
    1. Texas — History — Revolution, 1835–1836 — Juvenile
fiction. [1. Texas — History — Revolution, 1835–1836 — Fiction.] I. Wilson, Jo Kay, ill. II. Title.
PZ7.K7035Sar 1993
[Fic] — dc20   93-16171
                                                                      CIP
                                                                       AC

For my mother, Gladys Alexander,
a ninety-two-year-old Texas storyteller.

Sarah's Family

Sarah's parents moved to Texas from Christian County, Kentucky:
    Edward R. Bradley — b. 1760; d. 1826, Brazoria County, Texas
    Elizabeth (Liza) Bradley — b. 1776; d. 1843, Brazoria County, Texas

Sarah and her brothers and sisters were born in Kentucky. In about 1822, eight of them moved to Texas:
    Mary (Polly) Bradley Tally — b. 1798
    Thomas W. Bradley — b. 1799
    Elizabeth Bradley Winn — b. 1801 (remained in Kentucky)
    Nancy Bradley Gorbet — b. 1803
    John W. Bradley — b. 1805
    Edward Bradley — b. 1807
    Letitia Bradley Gates Bullock — b. 1809
    Sarah Rudolph Bradley Dodson — b. 1812
    George T. Dodson — b. 1820
Sarah married on May 17, 1835, in Brazoria County, Texas:
    Archelaus (Archie) Bynum Dodson — b. 1807, North Carolina; d. 1898, Live Oak County, Texas
    Sarah Rudolph Bradley Dodson — b. 1812, Kentucky; d. 1848, Grimes County, Texas

Sarah and Archie Dodson had six children:
    Maria Louisa Dodson Quirl — b. April 9, 1836, during the Texas Runaway Scrape
    Elizabeth Bradley Dodson — b. February 13, 1838
    Milton Milam Dodson — b. March 31, 1839, in Fort Bend County, Texas
    Harriet Houston Dodson McWhorter — b. January 19, 1841, in Fort Bend County, Texas
    Sarah Belvedier Crawford Dodson Adams — b. September 4, 1845, in Grimes County, Texas
    Thaddeus Constantine Dodson — b. February 2, 1847, in Grimes County, Texas

Contents

Preface

Many Texans give Sarah Rudolph Bradley Dodson credit for having made the first Lone Star flag. Of all the early Texas flags, her flag most closely resembles the official Lone Star flag that has flown proudly in Texas since 1839.

Sarah made a Lone Star flag for her husband, Archie Dodson, and other Harrisburg men when their troop rode with the Texas army in October 1835. The flag was carried in the war to win independence for Texas, but no one knows exactly where it was used or what finally happened to it.

The colorful designs of other flags from the Texas Revolution and the Republic of Texas can be found in reference books. They include Johanna Troutman's flag, the Mexican flag of 1824, the "Come and Take It" flag of Gonzales, the Texas navy flag, the flag of the New Orleans Grays, and others.

Sarah came from Kentucky to Texas with her parents, brothers, and sisters, perhaps as early as 1822. She and her family participated in almost every important event in early Texas. They saw Texas change from a Mexican province, to a nation known as the Republic of Texas, and finally to a state in the United States of America.

Sarah made the flag to honor her husband and Texas. But, as it has turned out, her flag creation caused *her* name to become well known in Texas. Sarah's story is a favorite of many Texans, including her descendants and many members of the Daughters of the Republic of Texas. Sarah's descendants who shared family stories with the author were Dee Watson Worley, Fred Watson, Doris Harrison Peters, and Carrie McKinney Burton.

Most of the people named in this book actually lived in early Texas and experienced the historical events related here. Details have been added for more interesting reading and to show the way many Texans lived during the 1830s.

The Bradleys in Texas

Sarah Bradley threw the blue ballgown back into the wardrobe drawer. It was the only formal dress she had, but was it fashionable? She needed just the right dress to wear to a Fourth of July celebration at her uncle's home. He lived on the Texas coast near the style-conscious Texas village of Brazoria.

The blue gown was an old one, having come to Texas by wagon from Kentucky. It was a beautiful garment to Sarah because she knew its history. Her sister Nancy had first worn the lustrous brocade to a reception for a Kentucky governor and to many other parties after that.

A beautiful dress, yes. But was it stylish enough for wearing in 1834?

At age twenty-three, Sarah had been in Stephen F. Austin's Texas colony for twelve years. "I've been here long enough to know that Texans don't worry much about how they look in their work clothes," she said to herself. "I also happen to know that Texans expect everybody to dress in the latest style at a party."

Sarah dropped into her favorite rocking chair and sighed as she stared through the open window. She looked sadly at the road that would bring Nancy's family to the Bradley home place in a few hours.

Sarah had worried about going to the celebration ever since the invitation came. She had been cross with her family all week, a great contrast to her usual quietly happy humor.

"What is my problem?" she asked herself. "It used to be that nobody loved dancing more than I, no matter what dress I wore. Now I seem to be doing everything possible to keep from going with Nancy to our uncle's party."

While helping her mother, Liza, clear the breakfast dishes that morning, Sarah made up her mind about the situation. "I plan to stay home from this trip to Uncle John's," she said. "There is just too much work to do here at home."

George, the youngest of the Bradley children, did not agree with that decision when his mother told him about it. He dashed across the hall from the parlor and burst into Sarah's bedroom without even knocking. His sudden appearance brought his sister to her feet, but her sad looks didn't stop him from pouring out his feelings.

"Hey, you can't back out now!" the thirteen-year-old said, pulling anxiously at her arm. "First of all, you know it wouldn't be any fun to go without you."

George's words caused Sarah to realize that this beloved youngest Bradley had never been to any social event without her. Sarah had willingly spent much time in caring for George after their father died in 1826. The brother and sister had developed a family bond stronger than most. Now, as always, the idea of disappointing George tore at Sarah's heart.

"Besides, I have plans for this trip!" George urgently continued his argument. "I want Uncle John Bradley to see that I have trained Arrow to be the finest horse in Texas. When he sees Arrow run, I know he will take me to enter the Brazoria horse races." After a brief hesitation, he added, "I also want to go to a shooting match. And I hope you won't tell anybody that you can shoot better than I can."

Sarah smiled at her brother's reason for wanting to visit Uncle John's family. She wished she could view the world in such a simplistic way and be thrilled about horse

2

races and shooting matches. But she was disturbed that George thought she'd brag about her shooting ability to anyone, male or female. Texas women were expected to know how to handle guns, but proper women wouldn't mention such skills.

Older brother Edward had heard George's pleas. He stepped in from the front veranda to agree with George.

"Mama will be fine, Sarah," Edward continued. "Brother John and old Callie will be here. I wasn't supposed to tell you, but our brother came over from his Fort Bend County plantation just so you wouldn't start making up excuses to stay home. Mama never likes to travel anymore, but we all think you need a change."

Edward stepped closer to Sarah and continued quietly in what she called his "lawyer" voice. "You and the doctor did all you could for our brother Thomas when the cholera took him from us last year. Your staying home from a party won't bring him back to us," he persuaded. "Any time now, Nancy and Chester will be driving up in their carriage to fetch us. Let's go join in the fun at Brazoria! It's time for you to step out some with other young folks."

Sarah reached out and hugged Edward. This gentle, bachelor brother had always been able to use just the right words to change her mind.

"I'll behave, dear brother," she said with affection, realizing she was being selfish in trying to cancel the trip. Then an idea made her eyes sparkle. "I'll gladly agree to go on the trip under one condition. I want George to promise to join in the dancing that is planned at Uncle John's."

Silence filled the room as Sarah and Edward turned to wait for their brother's promise.

George thought, *Maybe there won't be a dance. Maybe we'll all go to a horse race instead!* With that hope in mind, he reluctantly agreed to his sister's demand.

"Then I promise to enjoy the trip," she said, playfully pushing George and Edward from the room. "Now maybe the two of you would like to finish packing!"

3

At that point, she realized that she needed to get everything organized before Nancy arrived. Nancy was quite impressive by herself. Backed up by her husband, Chesterfield Gorbet, and their eight-year-old daughter, Julie, and ten-year-old son, Julius, Nancy had become the kind of older sister who usually gets her way. That "big sister" role sometimes brought out Sarah's stubborn side.

"If I want to decide for myself what to wear on this trip, I'll need to get everything packed before Nancy comes," she said to herself.

Sarah would travel in the nut-brown homespun dress she already was wearing. Like all women's dresses of the time, it was floor-length. She would cover the dress with a dark riding skirt to keep from getting so dusty.

To select other dresses to take, she went to the corner of her room and pulled back a curtain. Behind the curtain, her other four frocks hung from a pole attached across the room corner. She was fortunate to have so many dresses in this simple closet, more dresses than most Texas women had. Two garments were homespun cotton, and two were silk fabric from Brazoria.

For each rough-textured, homespun dress, it had taken Sarah two weeks to spin thread, four days more to weave the fabric, then more time to dye, cut, and sew the dress by hand. Such a garment was used for working or traveling. The silk dresses, one of dark blue and one of white, had been sewn by Sarah's own hands for special events.

She packed the rust-colored homespun dress, the silk dresses, bonnets, petticoats, and a dressy pair of shoes into the trunk. With the work completed, Sarah had time to think about her feelings.

The problem wasn't just that she still mourned brother Thomas' death. Sarah had many early years to learn about accepting death after her father Edward Bradley was taken from them. He died of wounds received in an attack by thieves along the road to the Texas capital at San Felipe. That was only four years after he and

4

his wife, Liza, had moved to Texas with eight of their nine children.

Sarah had learned more about mourning as she watched Liza force herself to go on with her husband's dream for their 4,000 acres. Running the large plantation meant long days of hard work for Liza and her children. In addition, Sarah had seen Liza suffer from living too far away to visit some of her children.

These experiences taught Sarah that Texas women had to be tough enough to go on with life. She always admired the quiet kindness her mother showed toward others, no matter what hardships came her way.

Certainly the problem about today's trip to Uncle John's wasn't that Sarah minded the thirty-mile journey through prairie land east of the Brazos River. She would feel safe from Indian raids or road thieves with the men and Nancy along, all experienced in handling firearms. Besides, she knew the trip would be magnificent, with trees, flowers, and birds dressed in their finest summer colors.

So, why fret so?

Just as she closed the lid on the trunk, Sarah finally realized the source of her anxiety. She felt out of touch with the times. That was it!

Because of her total concern for family, she had seldom held conversations with anyone other than family members in a long time. Surely she would be tongue-tied if anyone new even spoke to her! Uncle John's family would find her to be the dimwit of the family, unable to carry on a polite discussion, she predicted.

Then she heard Nancy's carriage coming up the lane. Oh, how much easier it would be to stay at home on the Bradley cotton acreage!

She need not have worried about the trip. As predicted, Nancy did take over for Sarah and the entire Bradley compound when she alighted from her carriage. Chester and the children followed her, carrying packages as Nancy gave instructions.

"Don't bother yourself about anything, dear sister," Nancy said and began ordering family and servants about with good humor.

As the last daughter in the Bradley home, Sarah tried to model herself after her mother, to show courage and dedication to duty. When emotions seemed to be coming undone, Sarah and her mother always just worked harder. Nancy, on the other hand, would ignore almost any problem and plan a party instead! She could bring laughter to Liza and could charm their old servant, Callie, with a big hug and a small gift.

On this July day, Nancy easily teased the two of them into preparing supper out back in the separate log building that served as kitchen and dining room. Hungry family members soon seated themselves on wooden benches at the long, wooden table. The furnishings had been made by Sarah's father not long before his death. Plans were made for an early breakfast at the same table the next day.

After supper, Liza and Callie began filling a picnic basket to be taken on the trip. Three of Liza's famous apple cakes would go along, one for the travelers and two for the Brazoria cousins to enjoy.

George volunteered to get squirrel meat for the picnic if John would go hunting with him. George's dog, Wolf, wagged his tail when he realized a hunt was planned. Wolf's job was to fetch squirrels that fell from trees after they were shot. Later, George would return to mold enough bullets for the travelers' supply.

Since the roads were in good condition this time of year, the group chose not to travel in the wagon pulled by oxen. Instead, Nancy assigned her husband and her brother, Edward, to make sure that the carriage and horses were ready for the journey. Then Nancy turned her total attention to Sarah, leaving few, if any, choices open. Nancy presented a surprise—a new calico daytime frock with small matching bonnet—for Sarah to wear in

6

Brazoria. The beautiful new dress took Sarah's breath away.

"You are truly a surprisin' woman, Nancy!" Sarah said, causing the sisters to hug each other and break into laughter at a joke that only members of the Bradley family understood.

Recovering from the laughing spell, Nancy inspected everything her sister already had packed. Nancy felt sure that the old dresses and bonnets could be freshened up with a new sash here and a ribbon or two there. A ballgown might not be needed, but the old, blue one had to go along, just in case. Dancing slippers were packed as well.

Just before sunset, George organized rifle practice out beyond the barns. For any journey, the Bradleys always practiced to make sure the guns were in good firing condition. As usual, the practice turned into a noisy, good-natured contest, with sisters challenging brothers.

George finally realized that his nephew and niece, Julius and Julie, were watching from behind a rail fence. With Nancy's permission, George invited the youngsters to get practice in handling firearms.

Like her mother, Julie found happiness wherever she was. She fired the gun when it was loaded for her, then laughed with excitement. Julius took a serious view of everything. He did not shoot the rifle until he understood how to load the gun with powder, wadding, and shot. After he fired, his excitement showed only in the sparkle of his dark eyes.

With rifle practice and packing out of the way, everyone turned in to rest before their journey began.

2

On the Road to Brazoria

Early on the morning of July 3, Liza, old Callie, and brother John stood on the veranda to cheer the travelers on their way. John held tightly to the rope that held Wolf, an unhappy dog left at home.

Nancy drove the two-horse Gorbet carriage, with Sarah riding beside her. Sometimes the children sat in the back. Other times they rode double with Chester, Edward, or George on saddle horses.

Nancy chattered almost the whole way. She brought Sarah up to date on matters of importance to the Bradleys and to all of Austin's colonists. Sarah listened carefully, in hopes this information might be of help if she carried on a conversation in Brazoria.

Most of the time, Nancy spoke happily of recent courtships, marriages, and new babies among the family and their neighbors. As was her custom, she usually left out references to hardships.

"We all have enough troubles without spending time going over the details time after time," she would say if others in the family brought up unhappy memories.

On this July day, however, Sarah could not help but notice that her sister sometimes lapsed into brief periods of silence. "Nancy, is something troubling you?" Sarah finally asked. "Is there anything I should know?"

"Well, I'll tell you what's on my mind," Nancy replied with a sigh. "It's mainly that everyone is so worried about our leader, *Empresario* Stephen Austin. You know he was the only one who would agree to go to Mexico City with a message from Texans. He went to ask permission for Texas to be a separate Mexican state, not part of the Mexican state of Coahuila.

"He should have been back from Mexico months ago, but he has been kept in prison. We wonder what is to become of him and this colony without him. Maybe the newspaper in Brazoria will tell something about Stephen." She paused for a moment before continuing.

"Those of us who were the first three hundred families to come with him to Texas know pretty well what is expected of us. But the families that came recently have no one to tell them the unwritten rules that govern us. Without Stephen's leadership, too many people are taking the law into their own hands.

"Even worse, Chester says no one understands the laws that have just come to us from the Mexican government," Nancy added despondently. "Santa Anna is president now, you know; and he has changed many laws. He threatens to change the constitution we agreed to support when we received our land grants."

Nancy pulled herself up straight on the carriage seat and reached for her sister's hand. "You know, we said that this trip was planned just for you, Sarah. I think it's really for all of us. We need this time together to remember the good things about our life in Texas.

"Now, I will not allow another serious thought on this entire trip," she said. She directed Sarah's attention to the prairie blanketed with yellow wildflowers. Then she began a story about the Gorbets' recent trip to San Felipe, where they had met an impressive fellow named Sam Houston.

On the long day's trip by wagon road across the Brazos prairie, loaded rifles always were in easy reach. The men rode close to the carriage, especially when approaching a tree-shaded creek crossing. Texans could never be too careful.

With the sun directly overhead, they reached their favorite stopping place for lunch beside the road. Nancy spread the lunch on quilts under the shade trees. The men looked after the horses, and Sarah went to get water from a certain pool on the nearby creek.

Although she was in familiar territory, Sarah carried her rifle as well as the wooden water bucket. She invited the children to follow her.

Sarah's long skirt made walking difficult along the bushy creek bank. She proceeded carefully, always watching for snakes or other danger. She pushed her bonnet back on her shoulders and out of the way, to be able to see in all directions.

The pool of water seemed farther from the road than Sarah remembered it. Briars tore at their clothes, hands, and faces.

I should not have brought the children on such a terrible trail, she thought to herself.

Julius walked carefully and silently after his aunt. He often led Julie, whose eyes were on every cardinal and every flower instead of watching for dangers along the way.

After what seemed an eternity, Sarah found the pool she sought, with water clear enough for drinking. In her first quick step toward the water, her shoe caught under a tree root. She suddenly pitched over, face down into the shallow pool, with bucket and rifle still held firmly in her hands.

Julie's laughter at her aunt's situation instantly filled the woods, as might have been expected. What was not expected, however, was a man's laughter.

That unwelcome sound brought a dripping-wet Sarah struggling to her feet. She still clutched the bucket and water-soaked rifle. Julius and his suddenly-quiet sister clung to their aunt's skirts. The three stood frozen with fright as they looked up the vine-covered bank. They saw a bearded stranger standing next to his horse only a few yards away from them.

The man was dressed in dusty clothes and a broad-brimmed, slouch hat typical of a Texas frontiersman. He showed no distinctive feature that Sarah would remember later, except, of course, for his blue eyes.

Years later, he would remember with amusement the sight of a very pretty young woman, soaking wet and looking determined enough to use her rifle at any moment.

He took no step forward, but called out to them. "I'm sorry I scared you," he said. "Don't worry. I'll get back on my horse and ride on." Almost to himself, he added, "It looks like other people have discovered my favorite pool of water on the way to Brazoria."

The three at the creek were too shocked at seeing the stranger to say anything to him. They didn't move until he had ridden away.

His final words drifted back to them, though. "I'm sorry I laughed, Miss. I couldn't help it when I saw you holding on to that bucket and rifle even after you fell in the creek!" His laughter could be heard again as he disappeared beyond the creek bank.

"We didn't let him get a drink," Julius spoke solemnly. Even at his young age, he knew the importance of water.

"Never mind," Sarah said angrily. "He shouldn't laugh at other people." Her manner discouraged any further talk. She filled the water bucket and led the children quickly back to their waiting family.

Of course, Julie ran ahead when they came near the campsite. She called out, "Mama, Mama! Auntie fell in the creek, and a strange man laughed at her! It was so funny!"

Family members gathered at the sound of Julie's laughter. Nancy wisely redirected their attention to the food. She knew everyone was hungry after the morning trip, and she could tell that neither Sarah nor Julius wanted anything said about the adventure.

The afternoon ride in the carriage gave Nancy time to force the whole story from her sister. Julie moved near to make sure that no details were omitted. Then it was Nancy and her daughter laughing in chorus, sending their happiness like music across the prairie.

Julius expressed no feelings from his seat at the back of the carriage. Only his eyes showed amazement that these two could laugh at such a serious incident.

Sarah talked of disappointment in herself. "Why did I bother to learn to shoot?" she asked, shaking her head in disbelief. "Just when I might have needed to defend myself and the children from a gunman, I fell in the creek and got the rifle wet." Then she added, "Since no one was hurt, I guess I'll have to admit that I must have been a funny sight." She was able to smile just a little before begging her sister to drop the subject.

Hours later, the travelers happily crossed the last stream to reach their uncle's plantation. Fireflies sparkled along the lane, and frogs were beginning an evening serenade. Sarah could see the silhouettes of her uncle John Bradley, his wife, Betsy, and their children, Johnny and Amanda. The four stood near a log house that seemed an exact copy of the home Sarah had left that morning.

Before all greetings were exchanged, Amanda gave Sarah reason for panic. She was well known for being unable to keep any secrets. Amanda announced, "You grownups are going to a ball tomorrow at Mrs. Long's." Then she pouted, "Since I'm thirteen, I think I should be allowed to go too."

Betsy Bradley quickly responded, using her good manners to cover Amanda's impulsive comments. "Oh, yes, we accepted the invitation for all of you. We thought you'd enjoy an evening with Jane Long and her friends. I hope that is agreeable to everyone. You'll find that you know most of the people attending."

"What a wonderful time you have planned for us!" Nancy said, in her usual excitement over a party.

Sarah felt uncomfortable, thinking about going to the dancing party. She simply smiled at Betsy, however, and said nothing.

An evening meal awaited them, served by lamplight at the long dining table. Conversation covered news of various relatives scattered throughout Austin's colony. Then Betsy talked about plans for the next day, the Fourth of July.

When asked what they'd like to do the following day, Johnny and George immediately selected riding and rifle practice. They invited Julius to go with them.

"This is only for boys," Johnny whispered loud enough for Amanda to know she wasn't included. He hoped his mother wouldn't hear because she would consider it rude.

"Are you afraid I'll outshoot you again?" Amanda whispered back in a teasing voice. Then she turned her attention to Sarah, who was sitting beside her at the table. She confided, "Cousin Sarah, I'm hoping to learn to shoot as well you and Cousin Nancy do."

Sarah was last to be asked what she would like for the next day. She directed her request to her uncle.

"Uncle John, please take notice of George's horse Arrow tomorrow," she said. "If you think Arrow has a chance to win, you might want George to enter him in a Brazoria horse race."

Soon after supper, the visitors were ready to be shown to their rooms. Sleep came easily to the tired Bradleys, even to Sarah. She was beginning to relax and enjoyed having Nancy make many of her decisions.

Friday dawned with a coolness from morning clouds over the Gulf of Mexico. Breakfast was hardly completed when the men and boys went out to observe George showing Arrow's abilities. Then they left for the racetrack to see about getting George a chance to race his horse.

Amanda and Julie were happy to stay at home. They even accompanied the women to gather vegetables for the noon meal. Betsy especially wanted her guests to see a new plant called a tomato. John had bought the seeds in a Brazoria store. He was assured that the red vegetable was not poisonous, as everyone previously believed.

14

Once, when Amanda looked unhappy because her mother said she was too young to go to the ball, Sarah thought of an idea that might help. "Betsy, will you allow Amanda to go to Mrs. Long's party with her cousin George as her escort?"

Betsy agreed to that plan, and she and her joyful daughter began to look through trunks in search of a dress for Amanda. The frock they chose was yellow silk, one that was still in style even though Betsy had worn it when she was Amanda's age. The long-sleeved dress had lace collar and cuffs and a full, gathered skirt and petticoat that reached well below Amanda's knees.

The men and boys returned from the racetrack in time for a late lunch. George was so excited he could hardly eat. Instead, he entertained the family with his stories about Arrow's performance.

"I'm really glad the track owners let me compete in a race," he reported, looking especially at Sarah, who had helped get him a chance to ride. "I almost won! With a little more practice, Uncle John says I can win over all the other horses!"

After lunch and an afternoon rest, it was at last time to dress for the ball. Julie, Julius, and their cousin Johnny looked forward to the games they were going to play while staying at home with servants.

"Would you like to see my ballgown, Amanda?" Sarah called to the next room where Amanda was getting dressed in the yellow gown. "It came all the way from Kentucky. You can tell me if it's what I should wear in your town."

The invitation was exactly what Amanda needed. "Oh, it's so beautiful," she exclaimed at seeing the blue dress laid out on the bed. "Cousin Sarah, might I wear it someday, too, when I'm old enough?"

"Of course you may!" Sarah assured her, slipping into the dress and standing before the mirror.

With Amanda helping with the dress fasteners, Sarah noted something important. "Amanda, your hair is reddish-brown like mine. Your eyes are as gray-blue as mine. This blue gown must really have been meant for you and me!"

"Oh, yes! It's for us!" Amanda said as she gave Sarah a mighty hug. She ran down the hall to tell her mother about the blue dress and to see Betsy and Nancy in their gowns.

In hearing Amanda's excitement, Sarah found herself smiling into the mirror. She was definitely in a happy mood, almost looking forward to the evening.

Nancy came to give approval to Sarah's dress and to arrange her hair. "I like your long hair parted in the middle and pulled back, Sarah!" Nancy said. "Now, you need a little curl or two for a softer look around your face. With the back part of your hair done up in loops, we can add some blue ribbon. Then we'll be ready to go!"

Everyone gathered on the veranda to get ready for the drive into Brazoria. Sarah was pleased to hear compliments from everyone — even from George, who usually took no notice of fine clothes. Even though he was uncomfortable dressed in a suit, George was not complaining about taking his cousin Amanda to the dance or about anything else.

I promised Sarah that I would go dancing, he reminded himself. *I would have agreed to anything to get that chance to race Arrow!*

On the drive into town, Sarah thought about how fortunate she was to have a wonderful family, including a brother who lived up to his promises. She had no way of knowing that the evening would include another person who would soon seem wonderful to her.

16

3

A New Acquaintance

On the Brazoria ferry crossing the Brazos, just as the July sun was setting, the Bradleys could hear fiddle music coming from Mrs. Long's inn. They found many horses tethered outside the inn, some harnessed to carriages.

A few carriages were gaily decorated in red, white, and blue bunting in celebration of the Fourth of July. As the Bradleys made their way along the walk to the veranda, other guests were still driving up from all sides of town.

Jane Long, dressed in a white ballgown and wearing red rosebuds in her dark hair, greeted the Bradleys on the veranda of the inn. She called John and Betsy Bradley by name. She had no trouble remembering that she also had met various members of the other Bradley family who lived further north along the Brazos.

"Perhaps you don't remember me, Sarah," she said as she took Sarah's hand. "You were only a youngster when I stopped at your family's place soon after you had arrived in Texas. My horse had gone lame, and the cold night was overtaking my companions and me. Your mother kindly offered us supper and shelter for the night, although I know you had little to spare in those hard times."

A shadow of sadness flickered across Mrs. Long's eyes, noticed only by Sarah. *She's remembering her child who died that winter,* Sarah thought.

17

Then the sadness was gone, quickly replaced by the brave smile of a Texas woman who had survived much sorrow. This woman would play such an important role in Texas history that she would become known as "The Mother of Texas."

Mrs. Long gave Sarah just the encouragement she needed that day. "I must say you have become a lovely young woman, Sarah, just as I would have predicted."

Attention suddenly was drawn to the street by the arrival of a noisy party of young people. The commotion caused Sarah to linger near the door briefly. Other Bradleys passed on inside the already crowded hall and parlor.

Sarah saw the jubilant newcomers arrive in a carriage sporting a white banner that proclaimed: "Harrisburg Wishes You a Happy Fourth!" She noted three colorfully dressed young women. They filled the air with lively chatter and laughter.

Four equally well-dressed young horsemen quickly got down from their horses. They tied the horses to a hitching post and helped the women get out of the carriage.

Sarah tried not to stare at the fashionable women and, of course, was careful to barely glance at the men. Instead, she disappeared into the hallway. She could hear Mrs. Long exchange greetings with the group outside, all of whom she seemed to know very well.

Sarah rejoined Nancy and Chester Gorbet as they followed Betsy and John Bradley in a walk about the spacious parlor. They greeted friends in a much quieter manner than had just been witnessed outside. Amanda and George had gone looking for others their age.

Sarah renewed acquaintances with Mr. and Mrs. John Austin. He had founded the port of Brazoria and had arranged for boats and small ships to travel up the Brazos River to sell goods.

Sarah was pleased to recognize several other family friends, including the Robinsons and the Richardsons. Becky Robinson stood beside Sarah to renew their friendship and to point out well-known people in the crowd.

"Notice the red-headed young man over there with a number of young Brazoria women gathered round," she said to Sarah. "That's the young lawyer William Travis. My brother calls him 'Buck' Travis."

Politician Henry Smith drifted by to speak to the Bradley men and to give polite greetings to the women. After Smith moved past them, Mrs. Robinson whispered about him to Sarah. "I know you've heard that his second wife died of the cholera last year about the same time it struck down your brother," she said.

"You notice that Rev. Roswell Gillette is standing near Mr. Smith now. The first two Smith wives were sisters of the Rev. Gillette. We all wonder if Mr. Smith may be planning to take another Gillette sister as his third wife."

Sarah wasn't concerned about Mr. Smith's next marriage, and certainly she had no way of knowing that he would soon serve as governor of Texas. Her friend's gossip only reminded Sarah that life in Texas was really hard for women. She had seen graveyards scattered across the Brazos area where many young women and their babes had been buried. Texas was a land where doctors, or even neighbors, lived too far away to be of help when someone got sick.

Sarah's somber thoughts disappeared when fiddle music drifted in from an outdoor dance pavilion. Then her brief enjoyment of the music turned to panic. She quickly sought out the refreshment table, knowing Edward would be there, sampling whatever good food he could find. She took a firm hold on his arm. That was to let him know she wanted him at her side for the rest of the evening.

"Let's dance, sister!" Edward said. He started for the dance area before Sarah could disagree. "Amanda and George already have found the dance floor."

"I don't remember how to dance!" Sarah whispered frantically.

"Anybody can dance a Virginia Reel, and you must dance if you want George to live up to his promise,"

Edward told her. He peeled her hand off his arm and left her next to Amanda in the middle of the line of young women. He took his place across from her and next to George. The sly smile on Edward's face suggested a plan: If she were in the middle of the line, she would have to dance. She would have time to remember how to dance the Reel by watching those ahead of her in line.

His plan worked. By the time it was their turn, the four Bradleys didn't miss a step. They danced down the line as lively as anyone.

When the dance was over, Sarah was breathless and excited. She even exchanged a few comments with others around her. Edward noted happily that her hold on his arm was lighter as they walked away from the dance floor.

Almost immediately, a man across the hall called for another Reel. It was one of the men from Harrisburg. With Mrs. Long as his partner, he easily found enough people for another round of dancing.

Still appreciating the charm of Mrs. Long, Sarah watched her every gracious move. Only incidentally did she allow herself to observe the dancing of "Mr. Harrisburg."

The dance was over too soon, it seemed to Sarah, standing at her brother's side to watch the moving figures. Then Mrs. Long called for everyone's attention.

"Ladies and gentlemen," she announced, "on this wonderful occasion when we celebrate the independence of the United States, we have only one sadness. That is the absence of our beloved Stephen Austin, who has been imprisoned while laboring on our behalf in Mexico. It is true that we are thankful for the United States, where most of us were born. At the same time, we wonder how we can survive the trials ahead for us in this Mexican nation of which we now are citizens."

Mrs. Long then asked Rev. Sumner Bacon to offer a prayer suitable for Texas in such a time of trouble. A hush fell on the crowd as they bowed their heads and focused their minds on Rev. Bacon's sermon-like prayer for Stephen Austin and his colonists.

Later, as conversation groups formed around the dance area, Sarah saw Mrs. Long with the same man who had been her dancing partner. They had begun a walk around the side of the dance floor, smiling and visiting. Mrs. Long seemed to find it easy to remember everyone's name.

When they came to Sarah, Mrs. Long took her hand. "I don't believe you've met Archelaus Bynum Dodson," she said, carefully enunciating the difficult name. Then, she teased, "Actually, most people call him Archie Dodson. I know I don't need to tell you he's from Harrisburg. Probably everyone heard the commotion when he and his party arrived here today."

As was the custom then, Sarah offered to shake hands with Archie. She wondered later whatever happened to Mrs. Long or Edward. She was charmed by the manners and conversation of this blue-eyed young man from Harrisburg and seemed to forget about everyone else at the party.

Sarah kept thinking there was something very familiar about him, but she had little time to wonder about it because other round dances were called. Some she danced with Archie. Other young men also asked her to be their dance partners.

Later she and Archie made their way to the refreshment table. He liked to talk, using a more formal way of speaking than Sarah had heard before. In no time at all, she realized how much she enjoyed listening to him and talking with him.

Too soon, it seemed to Sarah, Nancy appeared. She announced, in her usual big sister way, that it was time to go home. As Archie visited briefly with Nancy, Sarah smiled to realize her sister had interrupted simply because she wanted to meet the newcomer.

Archie, Sarah, and Nancy moved to join the other Bradleys, causing the cousins George and Amanda to stop

their whispered argument. He was ready to go home, of course, but she wanted more dancing.

When Archie introduced himself, it turned out that the men had heard of him. He had served as a representative from Harrisburg to the Texas Conventions of 1832 and 1833.

Sarah later learned that Archie took the conservative side in the Conventions. "He voted for Texas to remain as part of the Mexican state of Coahuila," Edward said. "In other words, he voted the way Stephen Austin would prefer. That tells you he is not interested in starting a war any more than the Bradleys are."

Sarah's kin paid their respects to Mrs. Long on the way down the hall to the front door of the inn. An additional person also joined them. It was Archie, who walked with Sarah at the end of the procession to the carriage. He politely said goodbye to all his new acquaintances, told George that Arrow really looked like a fine racehorse, then disappeared back into the inn.

The four Bradley men on horseback escorted the carriage through the darkness, across the ferry again, and on to John and Betsy's home. Overjoyed from the excitement of the evening, Nancy had lots of energy for teasing Sarah about the new young man. Amanda laughed at Nancy's comments, while Betsy, always uncomfortable with teasing, tried unsuccessfully to change the subject.

Sarah felt no pain from her sister's jokes. She was busy sorting through the experiences of this special Fourth of July, 1834, in Jane Long's inn, set in Brazoria in a Mexican province called Texas.

Near the end of their journey, Sarah smiled in the darkness. She finally remembered why Archie seemed familiar to her. This interesting new acquaintance with the unusually blue eyes was the man who had laughed at her when she fell at the creek.

Oh, what fun to keep his identity a secret from everyone, especially from Nancy! she thought. *But I wonder if he recognized me . . .*

4

Planning for Change

July usually meant a little less work for the Bradleys. In that month they waited for the crops to become mature enough for harvesting.

Liza and old Callie had time for themselves since they didn't have to cook food for field hands. Liza spent more time studying the Bible, often reading aloud to Callie. The two of them also liked to tend flowers and other plants they had set out around the place.

George always put in a good day's work when he helped his older brothers. In July, however, they were involved in business matters and didn't need his assistance.

Early each morning, George packed some lunch and rode away on Arrow. He was happy to spend endless hours exploring the Brazos River banks, watching passing riverboats, or hunting wild game to take back for Callie to cook. He knew to stay out of sight in July, except at suppertime. That way, the women wouldn't think of any special work for him.

Sarah enjoyed spending her time in the sewing room, a shed room built onto one side of George's cabin, with oak trees shading the area. She could open the large, shuttered windows to allow coastal breezes to pass through. She carded cotton each evening and spun the cotton into thread each day. Sometimes she rested from her work, simply gazing out across fields of crops maturing under hot rays of summer sun.

Sarah often used sewing room time for deep thought about important matters. In August, her main concern was the land trade suggested by her brother-in-law, Chesterfield Gorbet.

"Something has to change around here," Chester said to the Bradleys, who were gathered around the dinner table earlier that month. "You know, Thomas used to turn out more work on this place than any two other men ever could. Now he's gone; and the field workers are growing older and slower in their work. John and Edward just can't find enough help for all the farming.

"We'll be able to use or sell a good crop of Bradley corn, sugar cane, and cotton this year. Next year's planting and harvesting will be more of a problem," he said. "I'm thinking you'd be wiser to change to raising more livestock. That is still going to be more work than you can imagine, but it won't take so many workers to handle it."

Chester's idea was to combine his land with the neighboring Bradley property for the livestock. He thought they all would prosper more if they worked together.

"It was your papa's dream for his family to have more cattle," Liza reminded her children. "That was one of his main reasons for wanting to come to Texas."

"We have to think about you and Sarah, also," Edward addressed his mother. "The two of you have too much work to do in looking after the needs of all of us and all our workers. You need to rest more, Mama. One of these days Sarah may want to marry and move to her husband's place. We have to think of a way for both of you to have time to do what you enjoy."

Yes, something had to be done. Sarah knew a change had to be made. She also knew that even happy changes were hard to face.

Sarah announced a plan. "In two weeks, before you begin the harvest, let us all meet here for a family get-together. We will have until then to think about this change in our lives. While we're together, we'll discuss the situation until we can decide what should be done about the family property."

For the gathering of all the Bradley kin, Sarah carefully planned meals and prepared sleeping places for everyone. John and Edward came with their sister Polly Tally and her family. The Gorbets arrived on horseback. Nancy used a side-saddle, as women generally did, with daughter Julie riding behind her.

Nancy immediately assigned older children to take care of younger children away from the adults. Then she organized the adults so that decisions could be made quickly.

With Nancy keeping everyone in a good humor and Callie serving lots of delicious food and strong coffee, problem solving didn't take very long.

Liza wanted to deed farm land to Chester in exchange for grazing land to be used in raising horses, cattle, and other livestock. The old Bradley home and barns would become headquarters for the men who worked with livestock. Liza, Sarah, and George planned a move to a new cabin nearer Nancy at Sandy Point.

Family business was happily settled just in time for lunch on the second day. As the meal ended, George came running up from the creek where he had given a picnic for the younger children.

"Some man's riding in from Oyster Creek," he gasped, out of breath from his run. "It looks like a stranger. It couldn't be another Bradley because all of us are already here!"

The men moved across the veranda and out into the front yard to greet the rider. As always, they made sure that a loaded rifle was near.

The women used the time to clear away the remains of the recent meal until Nancy looked more closely at the rider. "Sarah, it's your young man!" she called in happy disbelief, much too loud for Sarah's taste.

The comment caused women and children to move quietly out to the veranda and down the front steps.

Before much more time had passed, Sarah, too, followed the others. She was close enough to see that, except for his old hat, Archie was dressed better than when she first saw him at the creek. He removed the dusty, slouch hat from his head as Nancy began to introduce him to Bradleys he hadn't met.

"This is Archie Dodson," Nancy said to her family. "He served twice as a representative from Harrisburg and always voted in support of Stephen Austin."

In introducing him to her mother, Nancy gave more information. "We all had the pleasure of meeting Archie at the July ball in Brazoria."

Archie explained to Liza that he was on his way from Harrisburg to Brazoria to represent his Harrisburg sawmill employer. "I hope that I have not come at an inconvenient time," he said in his usual formal way.

"You are welcome here," Liza said politely. She suspected there was something more special about this blue-eyed man than anyone had mentioned to her.

Finally, Nancy guided Archie toward Sarah, standing at the foot of the veranda steps behind all the others. "I believe the two of you met in Brazoria," Nancy said, then managed to direct all the others quickly away from the front yard.

As the family disappeared, Sarah heard Julie say to Nancy, "I know I've seen that man somewhere before! No one could forget such an ugly, old hat." Then Sarah and Archie were left alone to make polite conversation.

Before candle lighting time, Liza invited Archie to join her family in a prayer service. Prayers were given for Texas, for the safe return of Stephen Austin, and for guidance in following family decisions. A simple supper then was served.

George helped Archie care for his horse and invited the visitor to share his small log cabin. George had moved into the cabin several years earlier, when he decided he was too old to sleep in the loft of the main house.

"My cabin isn't very fancy, but you're welcome to it,"

27

George said. He sat on the side of a bed built into one corner of the room and directed Archie to a similar bed. "I hope you don't mind sleeping on a mattress filled with corn shucks. I inherited these two mattresses for my cabin when Mama and Sarah made new cotton mattresses for the main house. You also probably noticed the chairs that Papa made when he first came to Texas. He liked having Texas buffalo hide to stretch across the chair seats."

For another day and night, all the Bradley kin and their visitor remained at the home. Archie fit into all activities, going with the men to discuss horses and farmland, joining discussions about politics or business.

In the daytime, the children liked the slip-bark whistles and the spin tops he made for them. In the evening, they thrilled to his stories of Texas adventures, so scary that even George couldn't sleep after hearing them.

At dawn on the next day, it was time for Polly, Nancy, and their families to take the day's ride to their own homes.

Archie lingered a day longer, supposedly because George wanted to show him a new horse. The truth was that Nancy asked George to make up the story about the horse to give Sarah and Archie more time together.

Nancy and George had tried this kind of plan on other young men who came to court Sarah. Somehow, this time seemed to be different. While Sarah hardly spoke to previous young men, the two "matchmakers" were encouraged to see that Sarah actually carried on conversations with Archie.

"You seem to like life here in Texas," Archie said to Sarah when they took an afternoon walk down a wagon road beside a cotton field.

"You're right about that," she said with a smile for her tall companion. "The truth is that I love Texas as much as Papa hoped we all would. I looked forward to every day of the trip to Texas, even when we were afraid

28

of Indians. I liked Texas even when we were so tired that we thought we couldn't take another step."

Normally a person of few words, she stopped suddenly. "Oh, I'm sorry. I don't usually go on so. But, you're right. Texas is very special to me."

Archie answered immediately, "I know. It's that special to me too. It was good fortune that brought my father and me here." He sighed, shaking his head solemnly. "I'm afraid there is real trouble ahead for Texas, though. We need Stephen Austin now more than ever before. My hope is that he will get back from Mexico soon. He is the only one who can talk sense to everybody about living at peace in this Mexican state.

"Now I'm the one who must apologize," Archie said, stopping in the trail to look down at Sarah. "I am casting a shadow on this delightful time I have spent with the Bradley family. Instead of all this seriousness, let's walk down to Oyster Creek," he suggested. "We can count the robins hopping among the palmetto plants along the way. Maybe we'll see a kingfisher perched in a willow tree over the water."

With that, the two young people left the wagon trail and made their own path across the Brazos country. Archie pointed out details of the fall landscape, as Sarah admired his many interests and his skill with words.

Near the creek, Archie stopped to look at Sarah with a mischievous grin on his face. "By the way," he said, "I have a question. Since you aren't holding a rifle or a bucket, you won't trip and fall in the creek, will you?"

Sarah gasped, not knowing how to reply. Obviously, he did remember that embarrassing day when she fell in the water. All she could think to do was to follow her sister Nancy's typical behavior and just start laughing.

It worked. Instantly, Archie joined in the laughter, making the incident on the creek a pleasant memory for both of them.

Nancy would have been so proud of me, Sarah thought later. *I guess she's right. When nothing else will work, you might as well laugh.*

Next morning, as Archie prepared to ride away on his business trip, he had a moment alone with Sarah's mother. Sarah had gone to the kitchen to prepare a lunch for him to take.

"Thank you for allowing me to stop here and get to know your family," he said, before continuing nervously. "I haven't said anything to Sarah about this, but I would like to come by again if you don't object."

Experienced in dealing with suitors of her four older daughters, Liza spoke in her kindest voice. "The family enjoyed getting to know you, Archie. Now, you'd better ask Sarah about her feelings on the subject. Her papa and I always encouraged her to know her own mind. She won't hesitate to tell you what she thinks."

Soon afterward, Liza and her sons shook hands with Archie as he stood with his horse outside the yard gate. They left Sarah to walk with him to the nearby road to Brazoria.

"Your mother said I could stop by again," he said, waiting to see if Sarah would encourage such a visit.

"My family and I have enjoyed having you here," Sarah said with her usual open honesty. "I hope you will come again."

As he swung into the saddle, her final words suggested even more clearly that his visits would be welcome. "If we've moved on to Sandy Point by the time you visit again, will you be able to find us?" Sarah asked with real concern in her voice.

"I know the Sandy Point roads very well," he said, smiling and putting on the awful, old, slouch hat. Then, with a wave of his hand, he and his horse disappeared southward through a grove of post oaks.

A Mind of Her Own

Family members spent weeks of heavy toil in late summer. They and their workers harvested the crops and stored what they needed at their homes. The rest was sold at Brazoria or traded for flour, salt, and farm equipment.

When Sarah wasn't helping with meals for the field workers, she had other work to do, mainly in the sewing room. This time, in this room where she did her best thinking, the subject of her thoughts was Archie. After remembering every word he had spoken, Sarah had an important question in her mind.

Why am I spending so much time thinking about Archie? she wondered. *I've never wasted even five minutes thinking about any of the other young men who wanted to come courting.*

Then she realized how much she missed her father. She wished she could talk to Papa, so that he could give her good advice about Archie. But Papa had been gone almost ten years, and there was really no one else she thought would understand.

From her window in the sewing room, she could see a place that had been special to her father. It was an old wagon seat now located under the largest Bradley live oak tree. Sarah could remember, years earlier, how her papa looked as he took his turn at driving the wagon to Texas. Sarah was ten years old when she first sat beside

31

him on that wagon seat. Sometimes he talked as he drove. He always began with, "Pause and consider," from the Old Testament. After he had explained ideas that he wanted Sarah to "pause and consider," he would ask for her opinion.

Once she replied, innocently, "Well, tell me what I am supposed to think, Papa."

He was very upset. "Sarah, you have to look at both sides of any subject. Then you make up your own mind. You don't need to let anyone tell you what to think or what to do."

After that, she gave her opinion when asked and tried to have a reason to support it, just in case Papa asked for that too.

Usually, though, they sang together as they sat on the wagon seat. Their music flowed across the land as they made slow progress toward Texas.

Then they settled into their Brazos home, with enough room for everyone inside the log cabins. Soon, no one needed to use the covered wagon as a sleeping place or for storage. That was when Papa dragged the seat out of the wagon to set it under the big tree. It was a sturdy, bench-like seat with a back, made of heavy lumber to withstand lots of wear.

At the end of a hard day's work, after supper, Papa would sit out there. He enjoyed resting and looking down toward Oyster Creek. Sometimes he took his whittling knife with him to make wooden spoons and forks for the Bradley kitchen.

Papa was sixty-two years old when he arrived in Texas, and his family worried about his working too hard. Liza always wanted someone with him in case he started feeling sick. If Liza saw him go out to the old bench, she'd say, "Sarah, go sit and talk to Papa. I'll come as soon as I finish the work here in the kitchen."

He'd talk to Sarah for a while, always noting the beauty of the day and the wonders of Texas. Often he'd give bits of wisdom that had come into his mind.

Then he'd start singing in his magnificent voice. He sang whatever songs came to mind, from folk songs to church hymns. Sarah's small voice could be heard, straining to reach the volume of Papa's. Other members of the family usually came to sit around Papa and Sarah. They always arrived in time to join in singing "Amazing Grace." It was Papa's favorite song, and he always saved it for last.

Before long, Papa began to refer to the old wagon seat as "The Singin' Place."

Sarah began to think that she should spend some time at the Singin' Place. Maybe she could know what Papa would have said about Archie.

That evening, when she thought no one else would notice, she sat on the old bench for a while. She even tried humming a few of Papa's tunes just to get her mind to focus on her problem.

"Now, look at both sides of this matter of Archie Dodson," she told herself quietly. "Then you have to make up your own mind. There must be more to this man than just his charming ways and sparkling blue eyes. First of all, he talks a lot. But I don't mind that because I like to listen to what he says. He has a good voice, easy to listen to. He reads a lot and thinks about what he hears other people say."

She "paused to consider" before continuing her description of Archie. "But after he talks for a while, he always asks me what I think. I don't like to talk a lot, but it's good to have someone listen when I do say something."

Sarah couldn't remember any other young man who could ever think of anything to say. Certainly none ever asked her what she thought. "Only Archie—and Papa—did either of those things," she finally realized. With that, she sang quietly through the first verse of "Amazing Grace," in case Papa's spirit was out there watching, somewhere near the Singin' Place.

After that visit to the old bench, Sarah looked forward to Archie's next visit, whenever that might be.

Meantime, she was content to continue her work in the sewing room.

One afternoon in September, Sarah was busily "dressing" the loom, preparing to weave a new coverlet for George's bed. Her concentration was broken when she saw George galloping wildly up toward the sewing room from Oyster Creek. She noticed his coming especially because it was too early for mealtime. She also saw that both he and Arrow were dripping wet, as if from fording the creek.

By the time George had jerked the running horse to a halt, Sarah was outside to meet him. She hoped that Liza wouldn't notice the condition of the horse.

"Oh, George, what's going on?" she asked, with disapproval in her voice. "Mistreating Arrow with fast riding or swimming the creek is the kind of thing that has always gotten you in trouble with Mama. Was this ride so important?"

"I just had to tell you where I've been," George stated with excitement. As he dismounted, he seemed unaware that he might have done anything wrong. "Tomorrow, you have to go with me. I told them you'd come."

"George! You can't tell people what I'll do before you even ask me!" Sarah had been through all this before with George. He often made promises for her without telling her about it until later. After a brief pause, she asked, "Who are these people? They must live across the creek or you wouldn't have such a wet horse and saddle!"

"They live on Robinson land, across Oyster Creek. They're just getting settled in that old log cabin that the Robinsons built," George said. Sarah realized he was answering some questions, while ignoring others.

"Their name's Moreno, an older man and woman. One of their sons, Ernesto, is my age. Their daughter-in-law is your age. I think she's real lonesome over there, even with baby Martin to keep her busy. Her husband is away somewhere. That's why you ought to go with me tomorrow, to see if you can make her feel better." Then he

34

added, using a sad-eyed expression that always won Sarah over to his side. "Besides, it's not good for you to spend so much time by yourself in that old sewing room. You need to see other people ever so often!"

Talking with George was always confusing to Sarah. She could never be sure whether he was simply getting his own way or was really thinking of her welfare.

"Well, it would be the neighborly thing to do," Sarah agreed. She didn't admit that she was allowing her brother to win the argument. "We can take them a ham or something else from the smokehouse. We'd call it a housewarming present, a gift for their new place. Meanwhile, George, you need to —" Sarah began to instruct her brother.

"Yes, I know, I need to go to the corn crib and get to work," he finished her sentence. Liza always sent him to shuck and shell corn as punishment when he mistreated his horse or broke other rules.

"No, I was going to ask you for a better way to cross the creek tomorrow," Sarah said. "But you're right. We're almost out of cornmeal. We do need some corn shelled and taken to be ground at the gristmill next week.

"George, you're too old to be watched all the time and sent to do work as punishment," Sarah continued in a quiet voice. "Now, you're supposed to be mature enough to know that Mama's rules make sense. Horses are the most valuable and important animals that a Texan can own."

"I know, Sis," George said, looking more serious because he liked the thought of being treated as a mature person. "You're going to ask what would happen if suddenly we lost all our horses. Then you'll start telling me about Texas when times were really hard."

"That is exactly what I wanted to say," Sarah replied. "It gets right down to this fact: having a horse in Texas is often the difference between life and death. You may need to ride away from danger or ride to get help for someone. You may need horses to pull plows or carry supplies. It

35

still can be a matter of survival even now, when life is easier.

"I'm sorry to be nagging at you, George," Sarah said. Then she added thoughtfully, "You were right about something too. You used your horse for another purpose, a pleasure ride. When we first came here, we worked hard just to survive. Now the hard work is beginning to pay off, and we need you and sister Nancy to remind us to take some time for pleasure.

"All of this talk means that I want to thank you for arranging something special for tomorrow," she added, with a hug for George. "I'm already looking forward to some time away from my sewing."

With that, a smiling George led his horse away to feed him and to get the wet saddle off. Work at the corn crib would soon follow.

Sarah, amused at her brother, walked toward the main house. She was sure Liza and Callie had been able to hear most of the episode with George.

"I believe our George is becoming a fine young man," Liza said, looking pleased. More of her teaching had soaked into her son's head than she thought. "He still acts foolish, then thinks about it afterward. At least he is thinking. Pretty soon, he'll start thinking even before he acts! And he's right about tomorrow, Sarah," she said quietly. "Please enjoy the trip with your brother and bring some comfort to the new neighbor."

The next morning, chores were done before the day turned hot. George brought Arrow and Sarah's favorite horse to the front gate. Sarah appeared, wearing her brown riding outfit. She tucked gifts of food for the Morenos into the saddle bags. Then George helped her onto her side-saddle, swung onto his own horse, and called Wolf to follow.

George knew a place for easy fording of the creek a short distance from the Bradley house. He always used it on days when he remembered to follow rules about keeping horses and their riders dry.

36

Brother and sister kept the horses at a trot along the old road that led from the creek ford toward the Morenos'. They talked very little most of the way. Then, just as they came in sight of the cabin, George stopped near the recently harvested corn patch.

"I didn't mention that the Morenos speak mainly Spanish," George said. "Do you think that's a problem?"

Sarah grinned at her brother. "It must not be. You and Ernesto seemed to have exchanged lots of information yesterday. Was language a problem to either of you?"

"Well, no," he said. "He knows a little English, and I know a little Spanish. Each one of us just kept talking until the other one seemed to understand. Besides, who needs language to know that he likes riding horses as much as I do?"

When the Bradleys arrived in front of the double log cabin home, Sarah could tell that they were expected. The parents, Juan and Maria Moreno, came out of the cabin first, introduced themselves to Sarah, and shook hands with both visitors. By then, a young woman holding a baby appeared at the door, with a boy of George's age standing behind her.

Mr. Moreno spoke rapidly in Spanish. He introduced his daughter-in-law Sulema, grandson Martin, and son Ernesto. The father spoke several sentences about his other son, Felix. He waved toward the west and made motions as if he were firing a rifle. Sarah decided that Felix must be in San Antonio de Bexar, perhaps in the Mexican army. She didn't think his family was happy about his being away from them.

Sarah asked George to bring the gifts from the saddle bags and follow Mrs. Moreno to chairs and a table under nearby live oaks. While presenting the packages from the smokehouse, plus a toy for the baby, Sarah spoke mainly English. She also used the Spanish words she had learned during her years in Texas.

The Morenos accepted the gifts with many expressions of appreciation in Spanish, with some English words thrown in. There was much laughter while everyone was trying to understand everyone else.

Then Sarah held the baby while she and Sulema talked about little Martin. Sarah heard that Martin was a good baby, three months old, whose father had never seen him.

The young mother's words about the missing Felix brought tears to the eyes of the Moreno women and Sarah. As she handed Martin back to his mother, Sarah thought, *George was right about our understanding each other. Who needs language to know that we love babies and we want our family with us, safe at home?*

George and Ernesto unsaddled the Bradley horses and tied them to a nearby rail fence before disappearing with Wolf. Since it was almost mealtime, the Moreno women invited Sarah to join them in the cabin used as a kitchen.

A delightful aroma of unfamiliar seasonings greeted Sarah, and she wished for more Spanish words to ask about the foods simmering in pots at the fireplace. Without those words, however, Sarah decided to help by looking after Martin while the other women worked around the fire.

Mrs. Moreno called to her husband when the food was ready to be served at the kitchen table. Of course, George and Ernesto reappeared, just at mealtime, even without being called.

After the meal, Mr. Moreno and the boys went outside again. Mrs. Moreno carried her sleepy grandson into the other room, leaving Sarah and Sulema with some time together. They left the steamy kitchen to visit in the cool shade of the oak tree.

By midafternoon, the Bradleys returned home, carrying gifts of freshly made *tortillas* and a small clay pot filled with hot sauce. That evening, while they shared these with Liza, they told her more about their new neighbors.

"The Morenos had to leave Mexico because they sup-

38

ported the wrong leader in a revolution there," Sarah said. "Their friend, Lorenzo de Zavala, helped them find a place to live here in Texas. They worry about the safety of their son Felix because he is still in the Mexican army."

"They invited us back," George said enthusiastically. "And Sarah asked them to visit us. In the meantime, Ernesto and I have plans. We're thinking of getting rich by trapping wild animals and selling their pelts."

Liza smiled at hearing one more idea from her son's endless supply of exciting plans. More than that, she smiled because her children had followed the family pattern of being good neighbors.

Liza Bradley,
An Amazin' Woman

The Bible was read every morning and every evening in the Bradley home. Liza Bradley saw to it that every person in the household, whether child, servant, or adult, either read or listened to the reading at those times. Liza herself also studied the Bible during any spare moment throughout the day.

Few schools or school books were available when the Bradleys first came to Texas. The Bible was the only book owned by most Texas families, with only an occasional magazine or newspaper found anywhere. That was why Liza required younger children to spend even more time reading the Bible each day.

"You need to practice your reading," Liza would remind them quietly but firmly if they objected to her instructions. "When your papa comes in at noon, you can show him what you've learned."

If any quarreling developed among the children before Bible reading time, she would add another reason for the reading. "The Bible can teach all of us to deal more graciously with other people, including members of our own family."

A day never passed that some member of the family didn't find occasion to quote the Scriptures. Favorite passages of family members were quoted long after their deaths. On the Texas frontier, Liza found many suitable times to use her husband's favorite passage, "Love thy neighbor as thyself."

If Texas had only a few schools, it had even fewer churches. Those were located only in larger settlements like Nacogdoches, Bexar, and Goliad. In the first five years the Bradleys spent in Texas, one Catholic priest, Father Michael Muldoon, visited their plantation. Only a few preachers had come their way. Otherwise, the Bible reading and Liza's guidance were the only sources of religious training available.

Bradley family members always thought that Mama Liza was making prayerful plans for bringing more religion and education to Texas. Gracious and determined, she just had a way of making things work out.

The favorite family story about Liza's strength and determination explained how the Bradleys survived during their first year in Texas. Her husband, Edward Bradley, along with sons-in-law Chester Gorbet and David Tally, selected Texas land grants in 1822. They were among the first 300 families in Austin's colony. The men built a two-room log cabin on Bradley's land before going back to Kentucky for other family members.

The Bradley place then served as family headquarters while the Gorbets and Tallys built cabins on their own property. The Bradley cabin had a spacious sleeping loft for children. The "dogtrot," an open breezeway between two log rooms, provided more living and sleeping space for the many Bradley relatives.

Before leaving Kentucky, Edward Bradley had sent farming equipment and seeds by ship to the Texas coast. Then his family traveled overland in covered wagons, driving some livestock along with them.

After making their way across to the Texas cabin, Bradley and his sons immediately set off for the coast. The thirty-mile trip was taken down the Brazos River. They expected to find farm equipment and seeds where the crew of *The Lively* had promised to bury them.

The Bradleys spent a week searching for the impor-

41

tant equipment. They could find no sign of plows or seeds for the crops they had to raise in order to survive. After a terrible coastal storm set in, the unhappy, rain-soaked men gave up and made their way back up the Brazos.

They reached the Bradley cabin just before dark. Then Papa and Liza, their children, and grandchildren gathered to eat a very small portion of their scant food supplies. Never was there a sadder looking family than the Bradleys on the evening the men returned. The worried adults were able to sleep that night only because they were too tired and hungry to stay awake.

The Bradley wagon still had a heavy wagon sheet stretched across the top. Ten-year-old Sarah and several of the other children continued to sleep there. Very early the next morning, Sarah awakened to find Liza busily unpacking a large trunk that remained in the wagon. All the way from Kentucky, Sarah had wondered what was in that heavy trunk. But Liza had not allowed it to be opened until now.

In the darkness, Sarah could tell that Liza carried several heavy loads away from the trunk. Sarah began to help her mother take strange packets from the trunk to a place just outside the cabin door.

Liza said nothing about the objects to her daughter. Instead she started a fire, and the two began preparing breakfast in their outdoor kitchen. Busy with peeling potatoes, Sarah soon forgot all about the parcels. Then, as day began to dawn, Papa came out the door of the cabin and noticed a mound of objects lying on the ground.

"Now, what is this?" he mumbled. Then he began to unwrap package after package, moving faster and faster as he went from one to the next.

Liza left her cooking to watch her husband's actions. Her quiet smile was barely visible in the dawning light. Bradley sons followed their mother, viewing the puzzling activity through sleepy eyes. The Gorbets and Tallys also gathered near.

"Liza, what have you done here?" Papa asked,

42

astounded. He paused to try to comprehend what had happened. Three hoes, two axes, a small garden plow, and two large packets of seeds lay on the ground around him. That same ground had been so empty when he went to bed.

Finally, he rushed over to his wife and picked her up in a mighty hug. He twirled her around before finally setting her down again. Above the happy sounds coming from other family members, Papa's voice came through with a statement the family would forever quote. "Liza, you are an amazin' woman, a surprisin' woman!" he said, then hugged and kissed her soundly again.

The Bradleys and their neighbors knew Liza was "an amazin'" woman. No one doubted that she would think of some "surprisin'" ways to tame Texas, even when others had given up.

Liza and other women who lived along the Brazos often talked about having church services. Their main time for talk came when they were called to each other's homes to help during illnesses. At a neighbor's home, Nancy heard that Rev. Peter Fullenwider was holding a religious meeting in San Felipe. She just happened to mention it to her mother.

Without much delay, Liza and Nancy sent Chester to arrange for Rev. Fullenwider to hold a two-day revival. The location would be the picnic grounds on Oyster Creek, near the Bradley home. An invitation to the gathering went to all neighbors for miles around.

Only about twenty people attended the first time. Before long, however, Rev. John Wesley Kenney and other ministers began to make more visits to Austin's colonists. Whenever the weather was good enough for travel to an outdoor meeting, they invited people to the Bradleys' picnic grounds.

Such a meeting was set to begin the second week in October 1834. Rev. Fullenwider, a Presbyterian, and Rev. Kenney, a Methodist, promised to be there to hold the meeting together.

43

"We can expect more than a hundred folks to come hear these two preachers," Chester said. He knew that wagons loaded with children and adults would begin to arrive at the campgrounds early Thursday. All would be eager to hear the preachers and to have time for socializing.

Well ahead of time, Chester sent workers to make a brush arbor, a large sheltered area with its roof made of brush. The preachers' stand and rows of benches were set up under the brush shelter. Of most importance, he found a good place on the creek for baptizing during the religious revival.

Chester and his men prepared pens and feed troughs for oxen and horses that would be coming. He arranged places for wagons to stop and for tents to be set up. People would bring food supplies and cooking utensils from home because the women would cook every day of the meeting. They would find kegs of creek water and wood for campfires awaiting them.

Two places allowed for privacy. The one for women and girls was set near the creek north of the campgrounds. The other, for men and boys, was located near the creek south of the campgrounds. Both areas were partitioned off with quilts and wagon sheets hung from trees and bushes.

Liza's daughters and their families came early, knowing they all would play host to the scores of worshipers expected. A small, new Bradley cabin was given over to the preachers. The men could rest between services or study for their lengthy sermons.

People expected to share an early supper at the campgrounds on Thursday. That way, everyone could get to the brush arbor for the first sermon to begin before dark. Several large bonfires laid around the area could be lighted if night services ran late.

When it was almost time for that first meal, young George left the carriage at the Bradleys' front gate. His mother had not been well for several days, suffering from a serious respiratory problem that always bothered her in the fall. She would not consider missing the first services, however. She drove the two preachers and Nancy down the hill to the gathering. George followed in the wagon, loaded with food, blankets, and more Bradleys.

Only Sarah chose to walk to the event after all the others were gone. It was a lovely fall afternoon, and she wanted to forget all about the hurried work of the last few days. Walking usually helped clear her mind. She wanted to be ready to concentrate on the sermons she was about to hear.

At the yard gate, Sarah heard the sound of a horseman approaching. Even from a distance she could tell that it was Archie Dodson. She knew he had come all the way from Harrisburg after news of the meeting reached that village.

"It's good that you could come, Archie," Sarah said, her smile showing that she obviously was pleased to see him.

Old Callie appeared on the front porch when she heard a horseman. She led Archie to George's cabin, where he had stayed before. She provided wash basin and water while he unpacked and changed from his traveling clothes.

Archie rejoined Sarah on the veranda and walked with her down the hill. Sarah guided her guest to the picnic tables where she knew her family was likely to be. She saw to it that he had plenty to eat. At the end of the meal, she arranged for him to sample her specialty, Brazos Apple Pie.

Chester acted as master of ceremonies for the gathering. He called for the prayer before the meal, and later moved everyone toward the brush arbor for services.

Sarah and Archie were not the only young couple who were enjoying being together for the revival. When it came to a good place to meet a prospective suitor, a camp meeting ranked high. Probably most matrons at the meeting had met their prospective husbands at such a gathering back in the United States.

The custom among Liza's neighbors called for men and boys to sit together on one side of the brush arbor. Women and girls remained on the other side of the aisle. Sarah had some difficulty explaining the custom to Archie. Finally, however, he was convinced that they would have to sit with an aisle between them.

They had settled down on to their benches before Archie noticed that two preachers had been invited. "I'm not sure that I can sit still long enough to hear two entire sermons," he whispered across to her. His comment suggested he knew from experience that Texas sermons were lengthy.

The plain split-log benches with no backs did nothing to make Sarah comfortable. Sometimes her mind left the sermon. Her thoughts wandered to what she had learned about Archie during the three times she had talked with him. His good manners were obvious when he visited with her family and friends. Those same good manners now prevented his looking at his gold pocketwatch during the lengthy meeting.

On her side of the aisle, Sarah was careful not to glance toward Archie very often. It seemed to Sarah, however, that Archie listened with interest throughout the sermons. *I hope we can discuss all of this later,* she thought. *I wish I could know what is important to him.*

The final hymn was sung at last. Sarah and Archie were free to take the moonlit road that led them up the hill to her home. She took his arm to walk and compare their views on sermon topics.

Before long, Archie suddenly left the discussion of the sermons. "You know, we grow careless about Indians and outlaws that roam this country," he said. He glanced toward the dark trees at the edge of the Bradley clearing. "Moonlit nights have brought lots of problems to people I know."

"You're right," Sarah agreed. "We Bradleys always are aware of the danger. We have had friends killed by Indians on moonlit nights. But I also remember that

46

Mama gave us good advice, even as devastated as she was, right after Papa's death. After the funeral at Sandy Point, she said, 'We must go on with Papa's dream for us in Texas. We must go on living our lives to the fullest. We cannot destroy ourselves with fear of what might hurt us.' "

With those important thoughts in their minds, Archie left Sarah at her front steps and went on to George's cabin. Sarah joined her Bradley kin in trying to get unwilling youngsters settled for the night on sleeping pallets scattered along the veranda.

On the next day of the meeting, Liza's breathing problems were serious enough that she stayed in bed. Sarah decided to stay with her mother. She was happy that Archie returned from the meeting grounds in early afternoon.

They did what they could to help Liza rest easier, then went for short walks or sat on the veranda. They talked about what each of them wanted for Texas and for themselves in this new land.

After an early supper in Callie's kitchen, Sarah decided to take Archie to the Singin' Place. She didn't tell him the background of the location, but it turned out to be a good place for conversation. Among other subjects of interest, Archie told about coming to Texas with his father, Obediah Dodson. When Obediah died, he left his son the gold pocketwatch.

They were still seated when sounds of the revival singing began to drift up the hill. At first, Sarah and Archie just hummed along. When they heard the beginning of "Amazing Grace," however, both sang in full voice, forgetting about the revival singers. Discovering how well their voices blended, they paid little attention to the congregational singing.

The Singin' Place seems to fit him as well as it fit Papa and me, Sarah thought.

The last day of the meeting also found the young couple together for several hours. Archie enjoyed having

47

such a willing audience, and Sarah liked hearing more of the ideas and plans he had formed during his twenty-seven years of life. After talking for a while, he always remembered to ask Sarah about her thoughts. She carefully noted and appreciated this courtesy.

More often than not, however, Sarah would honestly say with her brightest smile, "You have said it just right. Nothing needs to be added to your remarks." She liked knowing that his ideas and interests agreed so well with her own.

Liza felt well enough to join them for the evening meal. She was not surprised to find a starry-eyed young couple across the table from her. They wanted her to hear their plans to be married in the spring.

Later, Sarah wondered if her mother had pretended to be sicker than she really was just to give her daughter time with Archie. After all, it was obvious that Liza liked him. Sarah knew this "amazin' woman" was very capable of helping things work out for Sarah.

Before the relatives left the Bradley home the next day, the couple announced their plans to marry.

"I hope you'll decide to be married in May," Nancy said, hardly giving the two enough time to finish talking. She took charge again, without realizing that she was doing it. "We can fill the cellar of your new home with goods from our gardens by that time," she said. She waved her hands to emphasize points and paced up and down as more ideas crowded into her head. "It will be after planting and before harvest so that everyone can come to the wedding."

Sarah interrupted her quickly. "We have chosen May 17 for the wedding, Nancy. I want to ask a favor. Will you help me plan my wedding dress? Of course, I'll want to sew it myself; but I need suggestions from you."

The family laughed. They knew that Sarah had made her request just in time to keep Nancy from planning all details about the dress.

Without ever noticing the laughter, Nancy hugged

Sarah and her soon-to-be brother-in-law. She said, "I will be so happy to help you in any way I can. You know I wouldn't have said anything about the dress unless you had asked me."

"I have one other favor to ask Archie, and you, Mama," Sarah said. "You see, I'd really like for us to be married here at this place. All our neighbors could be invited to the wedding. Will May be too late, or will we need to move to the new house at Sandy Point before then?"

The Bradleys all answered at once, but Chester said it best. "The month of May will be just right," he said. "The new house won't be ready before then. Personally, I think this is the best place for a wedding, if Archie agrees."

Archie looked pleased with the whole discussion. Holding Sarah's hand, he spoke in his formal way. "I join Sarah in asking for the honor of having our wedding here, where you began your life in Texas. It would be the best way I can think of to begin our marriage."

Archie soon left for home. He promised to return as often as his work in Harrisburg would allow. The Tally family was next to drive away. Then the Gorbets left, and Nancy was still calling out instructions to Nancy as their carriage turned into the lane.

"I'll be back next week," Nancy shouted back to Sarah and her brothers, who were watching from the veranda. "We have so much planning to do!" Her voice faded as Chester urged the horses homeward.

7

Letting Go and Moving On

Nancy spent a week with Sarah and Liza late in October. Sarah had a quilt set up in quilting frames. The three of them sat along the sides of the rectangular frame and stitched as they visited.

At first they talked about wedding details. Then, with gentleness, Nancy and Sarah discussed with their mother the move Liza would soon make to the new cabin.

Liza agreed to details her daughters worked out for her moving from the old homestead. Construction would start in the spring of 1835 on the new log home where Liza and George would live near the Gorbet property. Edward and the men hired to help him work cattle would continue to use the old Bradley place as headquarters. Sarah, of course, planned to join her husband at his home in Harrisburg after their marriage.

"The children are looking forward to having you near us," Nancy reminded her mother several times. "I know you will enjoy watching them grow. You've never been near enough to your grandchildren to see them every day of their lives!"

Liza seldom responded with more than a fleeting smile. Once she started with "It is so hard to leave," then changed the subject. She just wasn't ready to talk about her feelings.

In the winter weeks that followed, Sarah noticed her mother taking slow morning walks about the Bradley clearing. Liza touched each fence picket, each building log, as if to say goodbye to parts of her early Texas life.

On one particularly beautiful December morning, Sarah took the usual "memory walk" with her mother. Though separated in age by thirty-six years, mother and daughter were very much alike in many ways. For one thing, they were known for their few words and quiet ways. Also, they had trouble expressing their feelings. Sarah listened quietly when Liza finally was able to put some of her thoughts into words.

"It is so hard to leave this place, Sarah," she said at last. "You know I'm having trouble with this change, even though it was as much my idea as anybody's. It's just that all of this was part of your father's dream in coming to Texas twelve years ago. He saw that your brothers chose the right logs and cut every notch exactly right to make good, sturdy buildings."

Sarah listened as her mother retold the story of each plantation building, often using some of Papa's words. She explained incidents that had happened at each location as they learned to live in their new land.

"At first, the two log rooms had only one window space in each," she said. "We had so few windows because of the danger of Indian raids. Every wall of the house had shooting holes for rifles if an attack came. Spaces for windows faced the dogtrot, the open hallway that connected the rooms. Shutters covered the windows because no glass could be bought in the colony then.

"We set the spinning wheel and loom under the trees," she recalled. "The first thing your sisters and I wove was yards and yards of mosquito netting. Those Brazos mosquitos were so terrible at night when we tried to sleep.

"You remember that it took a while before the men had time to split logs to make floors in the cabins," she said. "Then the kitchen cabin and its fireplace were built. Callie and all of us were so happy when we didn't have to cook and eat outside anymore."

She looked around the property before she continued. "I wish your papa could have lived to see how nice the place is now. We have more log rooms, all with at least one glass window. He would have liked this spacious front porch that joins the rooms together. With good pens and barns for the livestock and more fields cleared for crops, we are so fortunate, Sarah."

That evening, the weather continued warm enough for the two of them to sit on the veranda and listen to the sounds of the coming night. After a long quiet time, Liza spoke again, indicating that she had begun to accept the change ahead.

"I am closing a chapter of my life, Sarah," Liza said. "I can only trust that more happiness will be ahead for me. I know I will enjoy seeing Nancy's children more often."

Sarah added, "Mama, don't forget that this old place still will be used by men who work on Bradley land. The place will continue to be important to us."

Liza nodded in appreciation of that thought.

The next morning, Liza woke Sarah and George just at dawn. "Let's get everything together and take a little trip," she said. "I want to see where that new cabin will be built!"

Sarah knew then that her mother had come through the hardest part of the change. She was ready to let go of the past and move on.

Callie had breakfast ready in the kitchen by the time the family was dressed for the trip. She was well into fixing a basket of food for the day when she announced, "I think I'd better go along too. I want to know just what we're getting ourselves into at that new cabin!"

The Bradleys agreed wholeheartedly. Callie would play an important part in making the new log house into a real home.

George and Sarah returned to the old Bradley place the following day. Liza and Callie wanted to stay with Nancy for several days.

The skies showed that a winter storm was coming from the north. Livestock needed to be herded into the pens and barns before it hit. Since John and Edward were busy at the Fort Bend plantation, George and Sarah would handle the work by themselves.

Sleet had begun to cut at Sarah's face by the time George stopped to talk to her. "Sis, I think we've done all we can to protect the animals. Now, you start a fire in the fireplaces. I'll bring in some extra water from the well in case this turns into a long, bad spell of weather."

It was dark by the time they sat down to eat the supper Sarah had ready in the kitchen. "I've tied Wolf on the porch so he won't get so cold," George said. "I'm planning to sleep in the loft room, where I can feel the warmth from the fireplace below. That will be a lot more comfortable than sleeping in my little cabin."

Sarah finished in the kitchen quickly and went to her room, tired from the day's work. She heard George climb the steps to the loft for some well-earned rest. Soon, Wolf began to bark occasionally, just enough to keep Sarah and George from dropping off to sleep. Then the sound turned to a mixture of barks and growls.

George knew there would be no sleeping until something was done about Wolf's problem. *He's always been a reliable dog,* George thought. *I think I should go find out what's going on.*

Clutching the rifle, George climbed carefully down to the dogrun. Wolf had his nose pointed toward the barns and continued a low growl. After a few minutes, George comforted the dog and reported to Sarah that he couldn't see anything wrong.

The next morning, a sleepy George untied Wolf and let him run free. The dog raced toward George's cabin. He barked and clawed at the door, then turned to sniff at footprints on the icy ground. When George arrived to open the cabin door, Wolf dashed inside to inspect every part of the cabin. With rifle held ready, George entered more cautiously, but soon saw that no human or animal was there.

Dog and master made further inspections of the footprints outside. George could see that the prints were made by two pair of moccasins that left the cabin some hours earlier. "Indians, probably Karankawas," he told Sarah. "The only thing I'm missing is the bear skin I used for cover on my bed. Otherwise, they must have just wanted some shelter from the storm. Now we can worry about whether they will come back and cause us trouble."

Before noon, Wolf returned from a morning of worry over the footprints. He continued to be as nervous as George and Sarah when the three went out to look after the penned animals.

While the Bradleys ate a little lunch, they heard a horseman coming their way.

"It's Ernesto," George called back to Sarah after he reached the front porch. "I wonder what would bring him out in this weather."

The two friends talked briefly at the front gate, then George hurriedly returned to his sister in the kitchen. "Ernesto says their other horse and two mules have been stolen," he said. "His papa thinks it was Indians that took them from the pen outside their barn. Ernesto's horse was in the barn, and they didn't take it. Ernesto saw a few footprints going toward the river, and he wants to follow them and get the animals back."

George finally said what Sarah knew he was about to say. "The Morenos can't get along very well without those animals. I want to ride with Ernesto, just while it's still daylight. Of course, I know that would mean you'd be here alone." He had the sad look that he always used to get his way.

"George, boys like you and Ernesto don't have any business going after Indians," Sarah said firmly. "I'll bet the Morenos didn't want Ernesto to leave his cabin to come here. You need to stay here, and Ernesto needs to go home so they'll know he's safe. The next time we see John and Edward, they'll tell us how to get the stolen animals back."

54

"Just until dark, Sarah," George quickly continued his argument. "Won't you be safe enough until then? Wolf can stay here to help you. Ernesto is going on to the river even if I don't go, and I just can't let him go alone. It would be safer with two of us together. I'm really a good shot, you know. Almost as good as you."

The last sentence was supposed to win Sarah for sure. "Yes, little brother, you and I are good with rifles. Yes, I could stay inside, holding my rifle ready in case I need it. No, it's neither safe nor smart for two boys to go after two Indians, riding those stolen animals. They are hours ahead of you, in country that may be strange to you." Sarah spoke with some anger in her voice. While speaking, she was stuffing a good supply of cornbread, ham, and jerky into two cloth bags. "Here," she said, thrusting the bags into her brother's hand. "I know you're going because you're hard-headed. I can only hope you and Ernesto won't starve before you find your way home. And feed both your horses before you go," Sarah said, always practical even when angry. "It isn't their fault that they belong to two foolish Texas boys!" With that, she disappeared into her room. George could hear her taking her rifle down from its fireplace rack.

While the horses fed at the barn, George and Ernesto garbed themselves in the warmest clothes they could find in George's cabin. They tied Wolf so he'd stay with Sarah, then made sure of their ammunition supply. Both saddles carried food, water, and ammunition. Ernesto also had a knife in a scabbard. He handed George one of the lariats from his saddle.

"We have to be ready to lasso the missing animals — if we ever get the chance," Ernesto said.

Moving southward, the boys picked up the trail from a few hoof prints in an ice bank along the river. "They're at least three hours ahead of us," Ernesto estimated.

From there, the two moved along as fast as possible, stopping only to search for signs on the ground. "They aren't slowed down like we are by having to look for somebody's tracks. We can only hope they'll stop for some reason," George said.

The boys were so busy tracking the Indians that they were surprised to realize that daylight had faded. It would be impossible for them to find their way home in the dark.

"As usual, I just didn't think about what I was doing before we got too far from home," George scolded himself. "Sarah probably knew that was what we would do. Now she could be in danger, and we're nowhere near to help."

Ernesto pulled his horse up under a river ledge. "We can stop here for the night," he said. "This will give us some protection from the cold."

"We'd better make a fire, even if it warns the Indians that we're here," George decided. "It will keep panthers and coyotes from bothering us, and we could use some warmth."

Ernesto unsaddled and watered the horses, while George made a small fire. The fire, along with Sarah's packet of food, gave them some comfort through the night. Neither boy slept much, however. At first light they saddled up and started out again to find Ernesto's lost animals.

They continued southward along the riverbank. Before long, both their horses began to act nervous. They strained to go faster.

"I'm not sure what that means," George said. "Maybe they can sense animals up ahead."

"Let's walk a while," Ernesto said, sliding down from his saddle and looking carefully through the canebrakes.

George did the same, walking quietly and feeling a scare building up inside himself. "I'm really not sure this was such a good idea, this fighting with Indians," he thought.

After they had walked only a short distance in the early dawn, Ernesto whispered to his friend. "Let's hide our horses in this brush. Then we can move ahead quietly."

"First, we need to load our rifles," George urged. Ernesto agreed that the time was right.

Another short distance and the companions saw the three mounts they sought. Apparently unattended and tethered to brush ten yards ahead, the animals were fifty yards from the Brazos River.

Looking past the animals, they could see two Indians their own age. The Indians stood barelegged in the cold river water, wearing only breechclouts, with small animal skins across their shoulders. They were dragging a deer from the edge of the river.

"The one with the long bow must have killed the deer with an arrow," George said quietly to his friend. "Then I guess he called for help in getting the slain deer to shore. He's got more arrows lying over there on the riverbank."

"There is your bear skin at the edge of the canebrake where they slept last night," Ernesto whispered. "The only weapon I see is that bow. I can't tell that they have any food with them except the deer. Maybe they're so hungry that they won't be watching for us." Then he had a plan. "George, I'm going to ride the horse and lead the mules away before the Indians can do anything about it. I'll use the reins that are on the animals instead of my lariats. Let's hope the mules don't get stubborn. You cover me with your rifle, then go back up the trail and get our two horses. We'll both ride away as fast as we can and meet on the road toward home."

Events happened so rapidly from then on that neither boy had time to be afraid. Each one simply did what his family had taught him about survival or what seemed logical at the moment.

With rifle aimed, George gave his friend the signal to go ahead. Ernesto crouched over to make his way quickly and carefully to the horse, keeping the animal between himself and the Indians. He petted the horse and whispered familiar words to him while loosening the tethers of all three steeds.

When the mules moved around more than usual, the

Indians looked toward them. They saw nothing in the dim light of dawn and went back to their work with the deer. Ernesto and George both froze for a few moments in their hidden positions.

Ernesto made sure that he had a firm hold on the three sets of reins before he made his move. With one smooth leap, he landed on the bare back of the horse. The sudden weight of Ernesto on his back made the horse stomp enough to make it clear to the Indians that someone was there.

George took aim and fired at the first Indian who ran toward Ernesto. Since George had to be careful not to hit Ernesto, the aim was off. The shot only grazed the Indian's leg and knocked him to the ground. The Indian realized his wound wouldn't allow him to catch Ernesto. Instead, he quickly dragged himself and his bow toward the sheaf of arrows to take a shot at George.

George knew he couldn't reload his rifle fast enough to outshoot that bow and arrow. He made an instant decision to get back to the horses that he and Ernesto had left on the trail.

When George fired his rifle, the sound helped Ernesto get the animals moving together in the direction of home. It was then, also, that the second Indian reached Ernesto, waving a tomahawk that had been hidden in his belt. Young Moreno made a frantic effort to spur his horse and kick his attacker away, all at the same time. Fortunately for Ernesto, the attacker tripped and fell over some brush on the riverbank. As he fell, however, his tomahawk made a gash in Ernesto's leg.

After that, the two Indians were left behind. Ernesto rode away from the fight as fast as he could get the horse and two mules to move. When he was far enough upriver from the Indians, he stopped to see about his wound. Soon George rode up, leading Ernesto's horse. George was disturbed to see that his friend had been hurt.

"I'm in good shape, considering what could have happened," Ernesto said. He tore a strip of cloth from his shirttail to cover his wound. "You know, I guess every-thing is pretty well balanced out today. One person was wounded on each side in the fight. They still have some deer meat to help them survive, and we have the horse and mules we came for."

Then the two sat without talking for a long time, rest-ing and reliving the awful moments of the fight. How close they had come to seeing someone die!

"I'm never going to get used to this kind of thing," George finally said aloud. "I like adventure, but I don't like this kind of fighting. It would be better just to use words if you have to fight. And speaking of words, I hate to hear what Sarah will say to me," George groaned. "I think you'd better come to our place before you go home, Ernesto. That way, we can be sure that she is safe. She will be happy to see that we did find your animals." Then he admitted, "Mainly, I want you along because Sarah won't fuss at me so much if you're there."

Sarah stood at the barn, watching for them, when they rode into the Bradley clearing the next morning. As they drew closer to her, they could see she didn't look angry. But she wasn't really smiling, either.

"I'm sorry we are so late getting back, Sarah," George said after dismounting. "I'm glad to see that you didn't have any trouble here."

Sarah didn't say anything at first. She just looked at her brother carefully to see that he wasn't hurt, then hugged him. When she saw the bandage on Ernesto's leg, she gave a cry of concern. After helping him off his horse, she hugged Ernesto too.

"I need to change that bandage, Ernesto," she said, after hearing a brief summary of the battle. She again looked at each of them carefully to assure herself that they truly were safe.

"You both could have been killed!" she suddenly gasped, tears welling up in her eyes. She hid her tears by walking quickly away toward the kitchen. "Feed your animals while I fix you the best breakfast you've ever had," she called back.

The boys could still hear her muttering as she went into the kitchen. "I wonder how Texas boys ever live to be grown! I'm supposed to be thinking about my wedding, not worrying about foolish boys!"

8

Wedding Plans

Sarah's wedding dress and bonnet would be copied from an illustration in *Godey's Lady's Book,* Nancy's favorite magazine.

"The dress must be nice enough for a wedding, probably silk," Sarah said. Nancy agreed. Before winter weather blocked passage across the Brazos prairies, Nancy had a peddler deliver blue silk fabric from Brazoria.

"It must be practical enough that I can wear it for many years to come," Sarah insisted. "It's also really important to me to make this dress myself, for this special occasion."

Nancy would have preferred something with more bows and frills. She had strongly suggested getting it made by a seamstress in San Felipe.

The older sister easily recovered from not getting her way on Sarah's wedding dress. Nancy's happy personality caused her to accept other ideas without much argument. In this situation, she simply moved her thoughts to other items on her list.

"I'll just let that seamstress sew your second-day dress and your third-day dress and some nice little bonnets," she announced, allowing no time for argument. "I've already found two lovely pieces of calico."

Nancy then took care of the rest of the wedding plans in a final statement. "Archie has been assigned to get an official from Harrisburg to perform the ceremony. Callie and I can handle all other details of the wedding day. We just don't want you to have to worry about anything!"

Making the wedding dress was the simplest part of Sarah's work in the months before her wedding. The preparation of goods for the new home was the most time-consuming and was very important.

Archie and Sarah would live in Harrisburg, in the small cabin that Obediah Dodson had built after he and his son arrived from North Carolina. The cabin had started out as a double log structure with a dogtrot. Since both Dodsons worked at the sawmill, however, they soon bought lumber for a back room and for a front porch. More recently, Archie had closed in the dogtrot to make a wide hallway between the rooms.

"When Father died in 1831, he was waiting for a land grant that Mexican officials promised him," Archie told Sarah. "If the grant ever comes through, it will be our property since I am his heir. Until then, we will be content with the little house in Harrisburg."

Liza invited Archie to come for Christmas week at the Bradley place. He was with them when they exchanged simple and loving gifts before the fireplace on Christmas Day. His gift to the family was a rare one in those days — packages of apples and walnuts, purchased at waterfront shops in Harrisburg. He also brought a new knife and scabbard to please his cabin-mate, George.

Sarah and Archie saved until last the gifts they had for each other. She had found just the right gold cufflinks in a peddler's pack in November and kept them for Christmas. Archie presented Sarah with a gold breastpin, a cherished memento from his mother. These gifts would be worn as wedding jewelry.

Edward announced another important gift for the young couple. "We want you to take Sarah's favorite rocking chair with you to your new home. It was important enough that Mama brought it with us in the wagon from Kentucky. We think it will have a special place in your family."

Then, it was time for Christmas dinner, featuring wild turkey and deer meat, vegetables from cellar storage, and fruit pies.

Soon after the meal, George insisted that Edward and Archie take him rabbit hunting. He said he wanted to try out his new knife in dressing the animal. Outside, however, he confessed, "I had to get outside! I just don't think I can stand any more talk about plans for this wedding. That's all those women ever talk about."

Soon Christmas was over and the new year of 1835 arrived. Sometimes Sarah thought the months passed too slowly. She was eager to be in her new home. Other times she thought the time went too fast. So much was still left to be done to get ready for her new life.

Archie described the house and its furnishings to Sarah and Liza. With no female relatives to offer advice, he asked Liza to give suggestions about furnishings to improve the place. He knew to prepare a cellar and a pantry to store food goods that Sarah and her family were planning.

While preparing the food, including smoked meats, dried fruit, and seeds to plant in their garden, Liza often cautioned Sarah, "You must continue to be very saving with everything. We learned to avoid waste when we first came to Texas. Your husband will provide for you well enough if you are careful with what you have."

Using tallow saved from beef cooked in the kitchen, Sarah made a supply of candles for the Dodson home. She and her mother also spent much time spinning thread and weaving fabric for household linen. Liza suspected linens were scarce in the Harrisburg house since only menfolk had lived there.

"In a bachelor's house, you can expect to find a good supply of rifles and muddy boots," Liza assured her daughter. "I doubt that you'll find many tablecloths or curtains."

Bradley livestock included a good number of hogs. On a cold day in February, the Bradleys invited Archie

63

and several neighbors to join them for a "hog killing." They would turn pork into ham and bacon to be preserved with salt or in the smokehouse. The women knew how to render lard by heating the pork rinds to make shortening for cooking. Some of the grease also would be used to make soap.

Archie was happy to be invited to help with the work. He knew that some products from that day's work would go with Sarah to Harrisburg in May.

In April, Chester sent word that he was ready for the Bradleys and their neighbors to get together for a "house raising." They would work together to get Liza's new house begun at Sandy Point. The same announcement invited the women to a quilting party at Nancy's home to make a quilt for Sarah. The event was a festive one, as Nancy's parties always were.

When Sarah and her mother drove the carriage back to the Bradley plantation, both of them were very happy. Liza obviously was looking forward to living in her new home. Sarah was elated over the new quilt. The women at the party also had showered her with more linens for her home. In addition, Sarah had received the two new dresses that were gifts from Nancy.

Sarah rode over to the Moreno place in late April to see Sulema one last time before moving to Harrisburg. In the months since the Bradleys met the Morenos, Sarah and Sulema, escorted by George and Ernesto, had visited each other several times. George went along on this trip, of course, but he was not in his usual happy mood.

"My face hurts, Sarah!" he said. "My hands are so swollen I can hardly hold the reins! And look at poor Wolf. He keeps rubbing his ears with his paws."

"I know you and Wolf both must feel terrible, dear brother," she sympathized. "You took more than fifty stings from those honey bees before you managed to rob their tree. It took real courage to get that fresh honey, even when you knew you were going to get bee stings. All I can promise is that I will see that you get lots of cakes sweetened with that honey. I'll be sure to use it in my wedding cake," Sarah said.

When they arrived in front of the Moreno cabin, only Ernesto came to greet them. At first, he carefully avoided looking at Sarah. Before long, though, she realized that he wanted to hide his face and hands, as swollen as George's. Obviously, their love of adventure and sweet cakes had inspired them to attack the bee tree together.

Sulema welcomed Sarah to the kitchen, where she had begun making candles from beeswax. At the hearth, Sarah could see a large pot of fresh honey, a gift to his family from courageous Ernesto.

"I have two surprises for you today," Sulema told her when they were settled at the kitchen table. "First, I have a wedding gift for you." She brought from a shelf a small package that held a shawl made of white lace. "We call it a *mantilla*," Sulema said. She showed Sarah the way it was worn as a headpiece in Mexico.

"I've never had anything so pretty!" Sarah said, jumping up to try it on.

"Now, another surprise," Sulema said, her dark eyes sparkling. She walked quickly to the back door and motioned to someone.

A young man in uniform came into the kitchen. He was carrying Martin. "Sarah Bradley, this is my husband, Felix. We have him with us for only a few days before he goes with the Mexican army to Anahuac. At least he will have time to get acquainted with his son." Sulema reached a gentle hand to touch a scar on her husband's forehead. "He has been in battle since we saw him last." Then she held up the *mantilla* for Felix to see. "Sarah is going to marry and move to Harrisburg very soon. We are giving her this for a wedding present."

Both surprises made the visit something that Sarah would long remember. She stayed only a few more minutes, knowing that the young family needed time to be together. Sulema walked with Sarah to her horse and promised to come with her family to the wedding.

George reappeared from the direction of the Moreno barn, carrying a small animal in a leather pouch. "It's a carrier pigeon," George told Sarah as they rode home. "I'll take it home, tie a message to its leg, then see if the bird will fly back to Ernesto. If this works out, we probably will go into the pigeon business."

The month of May finally came. Though she didn't believe in superstitions, Sarah awoke very early on the first day of May to try an amusing ritual. Someone at the quilting party had given her the idea.

She walked into the grassy meadow, brushed her hands through dew drops, and patted the moisture over her face. This should assure her of having a lovely face, exactly what she wanted for her wedding day. When she returned for breakfast, she laughingly told her mother and her brothers what she had done.

"You have enough good looks without May Day magic," Edward said. "However, today is a good time for you to have your wedding present from your brothers." He and George then brought in a large linen chest, made with Edward's loving hands. It was made from cedar wood that John selected along the Brazos.

"I helped Edward with it whenever I had time," George said, helping Sarah to fill the chest with her new quilt and linens. "The trouble was, I had to hunt a lot of squirrels this spring."

Sarah smiled at her brother. She knew that working on a piece of furniture would be punishment for George, just as shucking corn was. He was better at hunting squirrels and bee trees.

"I'll always remember that you were the one who brought honey for my wedding cake," Sarah assured him.

The day of the wedding dawned fair on May 17, with breakfast prepared for all who wanted to eat. A very nervous Archie ate only a few bites. He had arrived the day before and again stayed in George's cabin. George always hovered near, almost to the point of being a nuisance. Still, Archie felt comforted to know that Sarah's family members, including George, seemed to like him.

66

"George, will you do something really important for me?" Archie asked. "Will you bring the carriage around front when we're ready to leave for Harrisburg tomorrow?"

"You can rely on me," George said. He immediately went to make sure that horses and carriage were ready for the trip. As Archie had planned, George's absence gave him time alone in the cabin to settle his nerves and get dressed for the wedding ceremony.

The families of Nancy and Polly also had come the day before. Morning at the Bradley place found grandchildren playing noisily outside. The men spent lots of time drinking Callie's coffee in the kitchen. Polly and her mother welcomed neighbors who began to arrive soon after noon.

In early afternoon Nancy busied herself with helping the bride get dressed in her blue silk wedding dress. Instead of a bonnet, Sarah chose to wear the lace shawl, Sulema's gift, draped around her head and shoulders.

"You're an amazin' woman, Sarah, a magnificent woman!" Nancy said when the bride stood ready for the ceremony.

Meanwhile, Liza was faring little better than Archie on this, the wedding day of her last daughter. When she wasn't busy with welcoming neighbors, she went out under the tree in the front yard. She wanted everything to look perfect at the spot where Sarah wanted to have the ceremony.

"Everyone can see better if we have it outside," Sarah had said. "Mama and Callie's flowers will make a beautiful background."

Liza arranged a small vase of fresh roses for the little table where the marriage documents would be signed. Then, with nothing more to do, she looked toward the Harrisburg road. She worried that the official would forget to come for the wedding.

Before long, however, George saw *Comisario* Edward Wray approaching on horseback. The man was allowed a few moments to recover from his long ride. Then he set out the documents and stood ready to preside at the ceremony.

Nancy assembled the family and visitors in the front yard. Everyone made way for the bride and groom to come down from the porch together and stand near Mr. Wray. He performed the "marriage by bond" rites as required by Mexican law. After the reading of the marriage rites, documents were signed. Mr. Wray directed the young couple to have the ceremony repeated before a priest at the earliest opportunity, as required by Mexican law.

With the ceremony quickly done, everyone had time to visit with Sarah and Archie and to enjoy supper served from large tables set on the veranda. Soon after the honey-sweetened wedding cake was cut, Sarah herself served large slices to George and Ernesto.

At the end of the day, the rare sounds of music came from the far end of the veranda. A fiddle player from San Felipe and neighbor Juan Moreno, with his accordion, combined talents to set the beat for old-time American dances, with an added Mexican flavor. The honored couple, their relatives and neighbors prepared to enjoy a country wedding dance, Texas style!

The next morning, family members gathered to see the bride and groom off to their new home. On this second day of her marriage, Sarah was wearing one of Nancy's gifts, the second-day dress and bonnet made of white calico with red-flower print.

Archie helped Sarah to climb into the heavily loaded carriage. He accepted the driver's reins from the hands of his very reliable brother-in-law, George. The young couple planned to move the carriage at a good pace, stopping only to enjoy lunch sent by Callie. They could easily reach Harrisburg before dark.

9

At Home in Harrisburg

Sarah Bradley Dodson loved her little home in Harrisburg from the first moment she saw it. Archie need not have worried that she'd think it too small.

It was late afternoon when they arrived. The roads had been dry, and no real problem interrupted their twenty miles of travel. May was a good month for a wedding trip in Texas!

After escorting Sarah through the front door of the home, Archie left her alone and looked after the horses. She went directly to the kitchen, her first very own kitchen. Archie had described it all well: dining table, chairs, side table, and fireplace.

One difference caught her attention, though. The kitchen table had a white cloth spread on it, centered with a small vase of daisies. Obviously, someone had kindly prepared a supper for their coming. This gift meant that Sarah could look forward to meeting a very thoughtful neighbor woman.

When Archie returned to see the bright table setting, he said, "This must be the work of Margie Ferguson. She has been waiting for you to get here. She is James Ferguson's wife, just down the road from us. We'll meet both of them tomorrow."

As daylight faded, Archie carried in several trunks and boxes from the carriage. That gave Sarah time to look more carefully at the other rooms of the house. She saw that Archie had prepared a rack where her dresses could hang in one corner of the bedroom. Back in the kitchen, she lighted the small lamp, and the Dodsons sat down to their first meal together in their house.

On her third day of marriage, Sarah dressed in her third-day frock and matching cap of navy blue calico. She fixed breakfast and finished morning chores just before the Fergusons came to call. The two young women immediately liked each other. Sarah could tell that Margie would help her get to get acquainted with others in the small village.

That afternoon, George and Edward drove up with a wagonload of food supplies prepared for the Dodson home. Wolf arrived with them. He especially enjoyed riding in a wagon and barking at other dogs they passed along the way. Sarah was one of his favorite people, and Wolf wagged his tail happily when he saw her.

The Bradleys also brought the rocking chair they had given to Sarah. With that in front of the fireplace, Sarah felt completely at home. She was happy when her brothers agreed to stay a few days and help Archie set everything in its place.

The following week, Archie returned to his work at the mill. Sometimes he was away from home several days at a time because his duties took him to other parts of the colony to talk with mill customers. Sarah missed him terribly when he was gone, but she kept busy. She had brought enough homespun fabric to make at least two shirts for him. That sewing, along with unpacking the trunks and visiting with Margie, helped pass the time.

Before long, Margie took Sarah along to a quilting party at a nearby home. In no time at all, the others realized that Sarah was an expert with a needle. Their compliments embarrassed Sarah, who had no idea that she was greatly skilled.

In the weeks that followed, Sarah had occasion to meet eighty-five-year-old Mrs. Moore. Sarah commented on the spinning wheel and loom in the Moore home. The

71

woman's arthritis kept her from using the pieces of equipment, but she insisted that Sarah try them out.

After that, whenever Archie had to be gone several days, Sarah spent much time at the Moore home. There she could spin or weave for her own enjoyment. It also was obvious that Mrs. Moore looked forward to visits from Sarah.

Mrs. Moore taught Sarah more weaving designs and shared several old quilt patterns brought from Georgia. Margie sometimes joined the other two, usually making lace with her tatting shuttle while they visited.

When Archie was at home, the young couple frequently went with the Fergusons to visit other families. Whenever men were together, they talked mainly about problems in the Mexican state of Texas–Coahuila. Often the men asked Archie about feelings of other people he met on his travels around the colony.

"Everywhere I go, everyone is uneasy about what's going on," he told them. "Some men want to go to war with Mexico; others want to wait and work things out."

Late in June of 1835, Buck Travis came through Harrisburg leading a troop of Texans. They were on their way to demand the surrender of the Mexican garrison at Anahuac, on Galveston Bay. Archie and some others from Harrisburg started out with the troop. The men were armed with long rifles and with a small brass cannon mounted on a sawmill wagon.

Later that night, Archie told Sarah and the Fergusons about the trip. "I went along with them about five miles to Vince's Bayou," he reported. "I stopped there to take care of some sawmill business. It took longer than I expected, so I just came on back to Harrisburg. I don't think I really belonged with that war party, anyway."

The following day the Dodsons and others saw Travis and his troop march back through Harrisburg. They brought captured Mexican soldiers with them. The Mexican commander had agreed to lead his soldiers out of Anahuac and back to Mexico.

"We haven't heard the end of this," Archie remarked as the Mexicans made camp at the edge of town. "What happened at Anahuac is going to come back to haunt us."

Sarah's eyes were focused on the Mexican corporal, who stood near his commander. "It's already haunting me," she whispered, then continued in an urgent tone. "That young corporal with the scar on his forehead is Felix Moreno, the husband of my friend. He will be in danger if he goes back to Mexico. We must get him away from the Mexican soldiers and away from those angry Texans also!"

"Sarah, we can't get involved in this," Archie answered. "How can we get him away from them? Neither side would listen to us if we asked for him to be turned loose."

"I know what we can do," Sarah said quickly. "You must ride immediately to Lorenzo de Zavala. He lives on Buffalo Bayou. The Morenos are friends of his, and he will think of a way to rescue Felix."

After more persuading from his wife, Archie did as she asked. He returned shortly before dawn to report to Sarah that he had left the problem in De Zavala's hands. "He agreed with you that Felix would be in danger in Mexico. He thought of a way to get Felix away from Buck Travis. He didn't seem to think the Mexican commander would object to letting Felix leave."

"Thank you for trying to help my friend, Archie. Now we'll just have to have faith in Mr. De Zavala," Sarah said. Finally, her husband was able to get a few hours of sleep before reporting for work at the mill.

At a community gathering in July, Sarah was introduced to Lorenzo de Zavala. A former Mexican official, he had fled to the coastal area of Texas after Santa Anna took control of Mexico. De Zavala freely expressed his support for Texans. Sarah thanked him for helping Felix Moreno and was well entertained with De Zavala's story of the rescue.

Late in the summer, Stephen Austin finally returned from his eighteen months of imprisonment in Mexico.

Immediately, word traveled through the colony that Austin would be honored at a dinner in Brazoria on September 8.

Archie didn't want to miss hearing the *empresario* speak at the event to be held at Jane Long's inn. Sarah was just as interested. She wanted to pay her respects to Austin, a family friend, and to visit again with Mrs. Long.

The Dodsons traveled on horseback to the Bradley home near Sandy Point. They gathered up various members of Sarah's family to accompany them to Brazoria. Instead of going all the way by horseback, however, they went to the Bradley landing on the Brazos River. They boarded a passing steamer, which carried them on a smooth, comfortable trip downriver to their cousins' plantation.

In Brazoria, more than a thousand Texans paid seven dollars each to attend the event honoring Austin. When he stood to address the group, however, they were saddened and shocked to see him so pale and weak. The change in him prepared them for his words against the Mexican nation that he had defended for so long.

"There is no other course except for Texas to leave this union with Mexico," he said. His sad but emphatic comment came at the end of his speech. "Go from here today and form companies of men ready to defend Texas against the dictatorship of Santa Anna. He has refused to support the Constitution of 1824 that should govern his actions. This was the constitution that we promised to support when we accepted our land grants."

Immediately after he stepped down from the podium, small groups of men formed about the area. Each group became intensely involved in conversation. Sarah and Cousin Betsy stood with the other women. They were frightened to realize that their husbands were among those men talking of going to war.

The day after the Dodsons returned to their home, James Ferguson made a brief visit. "Archie, we'll be meeting with Andrew Robinson in front of the Harris home this afternoon. You both will want to be there because you know we're thinking serious thoughts, perhaps about going to war." He left quickly to carry the news to other homes.

Stunned that decisions were coming so fast, Archie asked his wife, "What shall I say if I go to the meeting, Sarah? If we go to war against Mexican troops, where can you go for safety?"

"We can make plans for my safety," Sarah said without hesitation. She surprised herself when she was able to speak so easily. She knew that her security was much on his mind. They were expecting their first child in the spring.

"You have no choice but to go," she said, thinking that it sounded like her mother's voice giving the answer. "And I have no choice but to accept the responsibility of taking care of myself as my parents taught me to do." Then she added bravely, giving mental tribute to her father, "Pause and consider, dear husband. This is what was decided when our families made the choice to come to Texas. They all knew that nothing would be easy."

Somehow Archie knew that would be her answer. They both had faith in the words of Stephen Austin. If he said that arming themselves was the only solution, that must be the truth of the matter.

The Dodsons went together to the meeting at the Harris home in late September. Other wives accompanied their husbands too. The women clustered together while fifteen men went closer to the house to talk.

Andrew Robinson was a Bradley neighbor and friend of long standing. His family left Kentucky only a few months ahead of the Bradleys. Both families followed the Austins to Texas. And both would go to war for Texas if that were what Stephen Austin thought necessary.

From where she stood, Sarah could see that the men listened to Robinson for several minutes. After that, they made some decisions among themselves, concluding it all with a general cheer. Then they motioned for the women to join them to hear what had been decided.

Robinson had been selected as captain of their Harrisburg troop. Dodson was first lieutenant; Ferguson, second lieutenant; and the others pledged to serve as soldiers.

"We'll ride toward San Antonio de Bexar to help wherever we are needed," Robinson said to the women. "Texas doesn't have any uniforms to give us, of course. Each man will wear just whatever he has. We'll take our own horses, arms, and provisions, and serve for as long as we are needed."

Some young man standing out of Sarah's sight spoke up. "Captain, that Lynchburg troop has their own flag. What are we going to carry?"

Robinson was so busy thinking about horses and rifles that he was caught off guard by the question. He turned again to the women for an answer. "Well, ladies, what do you think?"

A quiet wave of conversation ran through the group of women. Someone made a suggestion to the captain. He responded to the suggestion by asking Sarah if she would create a flag.

"Of course, I'll be happy to see what I can come up with, if that's what you'd like." The smile on Archie's face told her that he liked her answer. She said to the captain, "I'll go at once to see what I can make that would be suitable."

The gathering broke up, with the men going to search out all available equipment. They would meet the following day to make final plans for the ride toward Bexar.

Sarah wanted to go home with her husband, but she needed to go to Mrs. Moore's sewing room. Sarah had nothing but white homespun at her house. Mrs. Moore had a supply of colored fabric pieces that would be needed to make a flag.

"What should the flag look like?" she asked before Archie went toward home. "What do you think the men would like?"

"I'm not as good with colors and designs as you are," he answered. Then he added thoughtfully, "It would be

76

good to have some kind of symbol of Texas as an independent state. That symbol should not be an insult to Mexico. Those Lynchburg men are just asking for a fight with the word 'Independence' written across their flag. After all, Stephen thinks we may still be able to work things out with Mexico."

While wondering about a symbol for Texas, Sarah kissed her husband's cheek and went on her way. She tried to appear calm to her old friend, Mrs. Moore, who was just opening her eyes after a nap in her chair.

As calmly as possible, Sarah explained her assignment. "What would be a good idea, Mrs. Moore? What would the men be proud to carry?"

Awakening slowly to this new challenge, the old matron had a fine idea. "I've always loved the flag we had before we came to Texas—you know, the red, white, and blue. Isn't there something about the old United States flag that you could use to get started?"

"Yes, that is a logical approach," Sarah said, trying to calm down to focus on the new idea. She would add this thought to Archie's mention of a symbol.

Continuing with her trend of thought, Mrs. Moore made a strong effort to rise from her chair. She said, "I know I have some calico scraps of red and some of blue around here. There's always plenty of white."

"Tell me where to look, and I'll bring the scraps here to you," Sarah said quickly. The old woman settled back in her chair.

Following directions, Sarah found large pieces of the three colors. She cut out a large square of each and laid the three pieces out on a table near Mrs. Moore.

"Now, let's just try out some different patterns." Mrs. Moore began pushing scraps around in different arrangements. "You could use the design of the Mexican flag," she said. "It has red, white, and green stripes where you are using red, white, and blue." She lined up the colors with the white one in the middle.

"In the United States, each star on the flag represents a state," Sarah thought aloud. "Why not have a single star on our flag to stand for Texas, here on the blue square that is next to the staff?"

"I think you've got it, girl!" Mrs. Moore exclaimed. "Now, take these pieces with you and go along to create something for those boys to be proud to carry!"

Sarah did just that, getting home in record time. She found Archie fussing around, trying to decide which firearms to carry. She stoked the kitchen fire, so that she could heat a smoothing iron for the scraps of fabric while she prepared an evening meal.

As she worked, her mind wandered to planning the supplies for Archie to take. *There's the bread I baked this morning. Some of that could be sent, along with jerky and fried pork. That would last until he kills some wild game along the way. He'll need a container to carry water, either a bag made of animal skin or a large gourd. What clothes would protect him from the thorny brush he'll ride through on the way to Bexar?* she wondered. *He'll wear his favorite old hat, of course. I wonder if he should take his wool cloak for protection now that winter is near.* Her thoughts brought more questions than answers.

She had helped her brothers prepare for long trips by horseback before, when they readied themselves for possible Indian attacks. "Getting ready to go to war is the same thing as that," she assured herself. She happily remembered that her brothers always came back safely.

The Dodsons ate their meal quickly, just as many other Harrisburg families were doing. Archie was anxious to get out to the barn to see that his saddle and bridle were in good repair.

While he was gone, Sarah began work on the flag. Using quilt patterns from her sewing trunk, she carefully cut out squares of the three colors. They measured just a little more than twelve inches on each side. She pieced the squares in a long row, with the white square in the middle, then worked a narrow hem all around.

Finally, she made the master touch. She found a star

pattern, cut out a white star, and stitched it into the center of the blue square.

When she was through, she knew it was right. She held it up for her husband to see when he returned from the barn.

He immediately said, "Yes, Sarah, that's it! That's Texas! You've done it just right. We'll find a staff for it first thing tomorrow. I know the men will like it."

"Is this flag so well done that you think I'm an amazin' woman?" she asked him teasingly. "Just like Mama?"

Archie knew the family story. "You're amazin', and you're surprisin'!" he said, laughing. "Who else could have thought of a flag that combines United States colors, Mexican design, and a Texas star to symbolize independence?"

The young couple turned from the creation of a flag to the seriousness of war.

"We have thought about what I need," Archie said. "Now, what about you? With men leaving Harrisburg, things will change here. I'm not sure you should be here anymore."

"Tomorrow we'll see what Margie and the other women plan to do," Sarah said. "I have not seen Mama very much since May. It probably would be good for me to visit her."

The next day the Dodsons stopped at the Fergusons' place on the way to the general meeting. Sarah carried her flag carefully folded. First, the two couples talked of the best arrangements for their families. It was decided to find an escort out of Harrisburg for Sarah and the Fergusons. Sarah would go to Sandy Point to be with her mother. Margie and her two children would go on to San Felipe, where Margie's parents lived.

Both women wanted to stay in Harrisburg until they could give their husbands and the troop a good sendoff.

Sarah then asked her friends to look at the flag. As she unfolded it, the Fergusons showered her with compliments.

"Perfect!" James exclaimed. "It is perfect! Archie, I can provide a proper staff since I'm the fellow who will carry this flag. But you are the one who needs to present the flag to the men. Get your speech ready. You're good at that kind of thing!"

Back at the Harris home again, most of the town's citizens had gathered. The troopers stood together some distance away; their wives formed another group. They felt encouraged that five additional men had joined the troop.

Sarah could see James whispering to Captain Robinson about the flag. He pointed to her and then to the staff that Archie now carried, with the flag still rolled around it. No one had yet seen either the colors or the star.

The captain called for everyone's attention. "Fellow Texans, Lieutenant Dodson will now present the troop's flag."

Archie stepped forward and unfurled the flag. Sarah heard gasps of approval from every side as Archie spoke with conviction in his clear voice. "Here is the flag for the Texas troops from Harrisburg. The single star is like Texas. She stands alone in her opposition to the autocratic government that Santa Anna has now established in Mexico."

Applause and cheers filled the air.

Two days later, on October 3, 1835, just at dawn, the little troop of Harrisburg men kissed their families goodbye and rode out toward Bexar.

Margie Ferguson's eyes followed the soldier riding at the head of the column. He was Second Lieutenant James Ferguson, proudly carrying Sarah's Lone Star flag.

Sarah Dodson focused on a blue-eyed Texan in a slouch hat, riding near James. He was First Lieutenant Archie Dodson, the man for whom she had made the flag with its single, white star.

10

A Soldier at Bexar

Captain Robinson's troop consisted of experienced frontiersmen who had traveled the narrow Texas roads often. They had no problem in reaching Atascosito Crossing on the Brazos near San Felipe before dark on the first day.

Knowing that Sarah had been safely escorted to her mother's home, Archie actually enjoyed the day's ride. Now the troop would camp a few days in San Felipe to allow time to trade for horses and equipment.

More volunteer soldiers arrived at San Felipe and asked to join the troop. On their first evening, Sarah's brother-in-law, Chester Gorbet, came. With him was Felix Moreno, the young Mexican soldier the Dodsons had helped rescue in Harrisburg.

"The Mexican commander didn't let Felix keep his army rifle," Gorbet explained. "Yesterday, on his way to join the Texas army, Felix stopped by my cabin because he wanted to trade for one of my rifles. I just decided we'd come on over here together and go with this troop. Felix practiced with his new rifle all along the way."

Felix grinned. "Soon I hope to be as accurate with this long rifle as my young friend George Bradley."

Archie and Chester knew that would be accurate enough. Both glanced around quickly to be sure that George and Ernesto hadn't sneaked along on the ride with Felix. "I suspect those two boys are plenty mad at all of us for leaving them behind," Archie said.

That same evening, a tired messenger rode into camp with alarming news. "There has been trouble in Gonzales," he said. "The Mexican commander at San Antonio de Bexar sent his men to Gonzales to demand a small brass cannon. The colonists used it for protection against Indian attacks and refused to give up the cannon. You might know, a fight started. The men of Gonzales won the fight, but you can bet there will be more trouble ahead. You men of Harrisburg ought to get on your way to help those folks. It looks as if a revolution has begun in Texas."

The messenger went on down the road, telling his story to anyone who would listen. Captain Robinson told his men, "I know we're needed at Gonzales, but we'll stay here for a day or so to be sure we're ready for what lies ahead."

Archie and Robinson watched preparations take on a more serious tone in camp after that. But the captain still worried about his men. "If the fight lasts very long, I'm afraid they won't have the clothing they'll need for winter's cold. San Felipe doesn't have much to sell us, and we don't have the money to buy all we need."

Meanwhile, Lieutenant Ferguson enjoyed his flag assignment. The time in San Felipe allowed him to carry the unfurled flag along the streets. He always was ready to tell a long story if anyone asked about the flag. He liked to start by describing Sarah in very complimentary terms. Much later, he would end by giving the exact words that Archie used when presenting the flag to the troop.

The day soon came for the Harrisburg men to take the road westward to Gonzales, ninety miles away. Robinson expected to join other troops there for the final march to Bexar.

Just out of San Felipe, the sky warned of the coming colder weather. The troop rode for a few hours with a group of men that included Stephen Austin. Robinson and Archie rode beside Austin to visit while there was time.

83

Lieutenant Ferguson dropped back in the line of horse-men to find someone else to talk to.

He chose to ride beside a man and his son. Both car-ried good rifles, rode good horses, and wore frontier cloth-ing and coats, all in good repair. Ferguson noted only one strange feature about them. While the father wore sturdy boots, the boy had buckskin pants that were too short, stockings that were unusually long, and new moccasins.

"The name's William Tom from Tennessee," the older man said in response to Ferguson's greeting. "This is my son, John Files Tom," he added, but the young man hardly glanced at Ferguson.

The lieutenant took some time to understand their names, since he thought Tom was supposed to be a first name. Then he learned that William Tom was an expe-rienced soldier from the War of 1812. "My son is named for a friend who fought and died in the Battle of New Orleans," Tom said.

Enjoying Mr. Tom's friendly ways, and trying to for-get the silent son, Ferguson felt encouraged to show the troop flag. Nothing interrupted their ride for a good while, and Ferguson had time to give his entire speech.

Then, with the flag story completed, Ferguson made a mistake. He moved his horse to ride beside John Files Tom, just to try to get the young man to talk.

"There's something I want to know," Ferguson began. He used as friendly a tone as he could on a fellow who wouldn't talk. "Tell me about those unusual stockings you're wearing."

It was the wrong thing to say. John Files Tom glanced at Ferguson with a look of shock and hurt. He spurred his horse and rode ahead, quickly out of sight. Ferguson was left not knowing what he had done wrong, while Mr. Tom roared with laughter.

"I guess it's my turn to tell you a story," Tom said, when he finally stopped laughing. "That boy is only seven-teen. His step-mama didn't want him to come with me. She told him he couldn't come because he'd outgrown his pants and was barefooted. Besides, she hadn't knitted him any heavy winter stockings.

"Of course, he figured out he could go to the blacksmith shop and get some rawhide moccasins made. But what solved his problem was that some girl heard of his plight and gave him her new, woolen stockings. The only way he could come with me was to wear that girl's stockings!" Tom continued. "He sure didn't want to tell you about that!

"But don't worry about him. He'd rather be wearing them than staying home," the father added, still chuckling.

Ferguson was thankful that Robinson and Archie dropped back to find him just about that time. Their troop gathered beside the road and rested the horses for a few minutes. Mr. Tom and his companions continued on quickly, since Austin was needed in Gonzales as soon as possible.

Robinson set just the right pace as he and his men continued the trip. He wasn't about to let a hard ride injure a horse.

They passed other groups of Texas men along the way. Some brave souls were walking to war, and some had horses or mules that couldn't go very fast.

Once a group of horsemen passed the Harrisburg troop, apparently in a great hurry to join the Texas army. "Those fellows haven't been in Texas long enough to know to care for their horses," Robinson shouted to Archie. "We may find them walking and leading lame horses by tomorrow."

Putting the embarrassing experience with the Tom family out of his mind, Ferguson soon thought about his flag responsibility again. He waved the flag whenever he thought the men would feel inspired to see it. He also brought it out for other travelers or for the settlers living in log cabins scattered along the way.

Before long, however, the north wind hit and soaked riders and horses with its icy rain. The lieutenant decided to roll the little flag up on its staff. He carried it, safe and dry, under his coat and next to his heart.

Two days later, as they neared the Gonzales settlement, they met several groups of people running away from the place. Some rode horseback, and some walked at a fast pace. When Robinson asked each group about the situation, no one had time to talk.

Finally, an older and calmer man stopped his horse long enough to answer questions. He obviously was a peddler, with sale items hanging from his saddle in a variety of sacks.

After giving some details, the man summarized the situation. "The Mexican soldiers demanded the cannon back. The Gonzales folks refused. They said if the Mexicans wanted that cannon, they would have to 'come and take it.' So far, Gonzales still has the cannon. But, because of it, everybody thinks we might as well consider ourselves at war with Mexico."

He rode on his way with a chuckle, amused over the cannon story. He also seemed absolutely sure that a smart salesman would run away from Gonzales as fast as possible.

The Harrisburg troop let the road take them to army headquarters. When Robinson asked for the commander, a guard directed him toward Stephen Austin.

Members of the troop dismounted and led their horses through the lines of about 300 Texas volunteers. No two men were dressed alike. Most were armed with bowie knives and long, single-barreled, muzzle-loading flintlock rifles.

Robinson finally reached the camp of the newly elected Commander Austin. In the excitement of the moment, of course, Ferguson freely waved the troop flag. Austin greeted them all personally, but he kept glancing at the flag as if it disturbed him.

In his usual polite manner, Austin said, "Gentlemen, I request that you not fly your flag." He turned his request into a command. "Not here in Gonzales, and not on our way to Bexar. It well might create more distrust in the Mexican leaders. They might think the Lone Star represents a demand for the total independence of Texas. We are facing enough of their anger without creating more."

"We'll do as you say, Stephen," Robinson said, then went on to the main problem in his mind. "Now, what we need to know is where we're supposed to camp and what we're supposed to do. The men of Harrisburg came here to fight, if that is what we need to do. Then we want to get on back home as soon as possible."

Austin pointed toward a campsite and said, "Soon we'll let you know where your men will be needed. We still have a lot of organizing to get done on the Texas army. Let your men rest until you have further orders." He returned to his tent to join several other men sitting in conference.

On horseback again, Robinson led the troop to the assigned area. After their days on the road, the men were glad to camp in one place for a while. Only Ferguson seemed unhappy.

"How come Mr. Austin didn't wait for me to tell him the story of our flag?" he burst out. "I saw other troops with flags. Now what are we supposed to do? Just throw it away?"

Archie decided to reason with his friend. "Let's follow our orders, James. Sarah would tell you the same thing if she were here. Take the flag off its staff, and fold it so it'll fit in your saddlebag. Let's just wait and see if a time will come for us to get it out again."

The words seemed to calm Ferguson, probably because he was allowed to keep the flag. When he had tucked it safely into his leather saddlebag, he joined the others in making camp.

The next day, Robinson and Archie spent time at headquarters to learn of plans for the volunteer army. Austin told them very plainly that they were facing war. "Retreat is now impossible," he said. "We must go forward to victory, or die the death of traitors."

Later, Robinson called his troop together to repeat Austin's statement and give them instructions. "Tomorrow we all will become soldiers in Captain Eberly's company for the march to Bexar," he said. "We'll still be together as men from Harrisburg, but he'll be our captain in the First Regiment of Texas Volunteers. We all told General Austin that we needed more equipment. He sent a message back to San Felipe to tell them to find us more wagons, ammunition, and provisions."

Austin's army increased in number every day, adding such famous men as Ben Milam and James Bowie at Gonzales.

On October 13, 1835, the army began the seventy-mile march further westward to Bexar. The "Come and Take It" flag flew at the head of the line of soldiers. The army's only cannon, the one from Gonzales, brought up the rear. It was mounted on wooden wheels and pulled by two yokes of longhorned Texas steers. Its escorts were men carrying homemade lances. Before they had gone far, however, the wheels wore out. The little cannon had to be left beside the road.

Along the line of march, Archie and other Harrisburg men rode behind their new captain. Archie was glad that he couldn't see Ferguson.

"If I can't see him, I'm not responsible if he goes against orders and flies Sarah's flag," he assured himself.

Late on that first day of their march to Bexar, the men passed a road junction. At that point, a large group of North Texans on horseback joined them on their ride.

A smiling, older North Texan pulled up to ride beside Ferguson. Everything about this man's clothes was strange, but Ferguson had learned his lesson from the Tom family. He wasn't about to ask any questions.

He didn't need to. The man introduced himself. "I'm George Washington," he said, with his eyes sparkling and a mischievous grin crossing his face. He waited for Ferguson to react to this impressive name.

Sure enough, Ferguson began wondering if possibly

this grinning man could be the first president of the United States. *Here is a strange person, dressed in top hat and handsome boots,* Ferguson said to himself. *He has a long-tailed, black coat over a fancy vest and homespun shirt and trousers. He's riding the biggest, fastest mule I have ever seen. He might just be anybody.*

After enjoying Ferguson's confusion for just the right length of time, the man spoke again, "George Washington Smith, that is! It's been a long ride for us coming a great distance from the Red River," he laughed. "You can't blame me for wanting to add a little humor to make the miles pass faster!"

Then he asked just the right question to make Ferguson his friend for life. "Say, boy, is that a flag you've got rolled up on a staff that's stuck in your saddlebags?"

Ferguson gave every detail of the flag story. He finished just as the troop reached camp on Salado Creek. It was October 20, 1835, and they were only fourteen miles from Bexar.

At Salado, they were visited by Sam Houston and several other officials. They rode over one day from San Felipe, where they were trying to form a government for Texas. Ferguson made sure the flag was in view, and he was disappointed that no one asked him to talk about it.

With the army increased to more than 600 volunteer soldiers, General Austin began the six-week Siege of Bexar. The Texans attempted to surround the little village, hoping to cut off supply lines to the Mexican army stationed in the center of town.

Slowly, as the days passed, the Texans made their way toward Bexar. They camped at Mission Espada, nine miles from town, for a brief time. Soon after that, the Texans were able to stop Mexican assaults against them near Mission Concepcion, two miles from Bexar.

On November 25, Austin returned to San Felipe, leaving Colonel Edward Burleson in command. The siege of the village continued through November. As the chill of winter settled along the San Antonio River, it increased the homesickness of the volunteers.

Archie wrote letters to Sarah and handed them to anyone he saw around San Antonio, stranger or friend, who expected to travel through Sandy Point. He didn't know whether she received the messages or not. He had not heard from her.

He heard the volunteer soldiers complaining angrily because they didn't like waiting for a battle. They were ready to attack the Mexican soldiers in the center of the village.

"We came here to fight for Texas independence!" they said. "Now, let's get it done so we can get on back home."

Ben Milam heard their words. He encouraged them to stay and finish the fight for Texas. "Who will go with old Ben Milam into San Antonio?" he asked.

With 300 Texans following, Milam and Francis Johnson led a five-day assault on San Antonio de Bexar. On December 7, Milam was killed in battle. Because of his bravery that day, he became one of the best known heroes of Texas history.

Remembering Milam's courage, the Texans continued the fight. On December 10, General Martín Perfecto de Cos surrendered San Antonio to the Texans. He was allowed to march with his men back to Mexico.

After the Mexican surrender, Archie looked around to find men of Harrisburg. Through the battle smoke and beyond the moving figures of men and horses, he could see Ferguson. He was on horseback, victoriously waving a red, white, and blue banner. Even at a distance, Archie could see Sarah's white Lone Star glowing brightly on the blue background.

After all he had experienced in San Antonio, Archie hoped there would be no more battles. He had seen enough of war. With the victory in San Antonio, the new commander of the Texas army, General Sam Houston, sent volunteer soldiers home. He knew the men were needed there to protect their families from dangers of frontier life.

"We've done all we can do here to gain freedom for Texans," Archie said to fellow volunteers Chester and Felix. "We can always join up again if we're needed." They saddled up and left for home.

11

The Runaway Scrape

Christmas of 1835 found Archie standing at the door of Liza's home at Sandy Point. He was a ragged, cold Texan, tired and emotional. For once, he had no words to say as he embraced his wife. He had been so anxious to get home to Sarah that he hardly stopped to eat or rest along the way.

The soldier revived after several days of rest, good food, and warmth from the fireplace. He found Sarah in good health, except for worry about him. The two of them spent many hours of conversation in front of the fire. They told and retold experiences from the two months they had spent apart.

"I'm back, safe enough, Sarah," he said, after recovering for a week. "But surely you've noticed that I don't have your little flag with me."

"It's so wonderful to have you here that I didn't think about anything else," she answered. "You briefly mentioned the flag in the two letters that came from Bexar. Now, since you brought it up, what did happen to the flag?"

Archie told of James Ferguson's good care of the flag and his feelings when told not to fly it.

"Then, on our way home together, I didn't see the flag anywhere," Archie said. "I asked James about it. He said he gave it to a soldier named Sutherland, who was staying on at the Alamo. I told James you'd probably think that was a good idea."

"Oh, yes! I like that!" Sarah said. "That single white star belongs there where you volunteers fought for Texas independence. Maybe we'll get to meet that soldier someday. He can tell us what happened to the flag after James left it."

Then she laughed and said, "You know, Archie, it was such a very small flag. It was so kind of James to give it so much attention."

Soon, Sarah wanted to move back to the old Bradley plantation, where many old furnishings remained in use. Unfortunately, the Brazos country was having the wettest spring that anyone could remember. The rain meant that Sarah seldom was able to get outside to enjoy the land she had loved from childhood. She stayed busy indoors, however, making clothes for the baby expected in April.

Archie planted corn and vegetables in a small field near the cabin. The crop would be large enough to furnish his small family with food for the year.

Like most Texans, it was hard for the Dodsons to know about events happening in the rest of Texas. Any traveler who stopped for the night at their place was expected to report on important news events.

In mid-February, Chester made a special trip over to give the Dodsons the alarming news he had heard in San Felipe. He also brought a copy of the San Felipe newspaper, *The Telegraph and Texas Register.*

"General Santa Anna is about to cross the Rio Grande into Texas," he said. "He's bringing four thousand Mexican soldiers to recapture San Antonio. Some of our friends are talking about going to Gonzales to rejoin the army, with General Sam Houston in command. I think we'd better wait a week or so before we decide what to do. We may be needed right here at home, instead of in the army."

In early March, the sky cleared long enough for Archie to ride over to see about his property in Harrisburg. As a surprise for Sarah, he hired a peddler to deliver the rocking chair back to her at the plantation.

Archie also brought back lots of news. On March 2, 1836, delegates at Washington-on-the-Brazos had signed the Texas Declaration of Independence. The document announced that Texas was no longer a Mexican state. Instead, it had become an independent nation, the Republic of Texas.

Other reports told about William B. Travis, commander of the small group of men at the Alamo in San Antonio. He sent urgent messages to the people of Texas, asking for more men to defend the Alamo.

Archie was in San Felipe when he learned that the Alamo had fallen to Santa Anna's army on March 6. "I shall never surrender or retreat," Travis wrote during his last days at the Alamo. "God and Texas! Victory or death!"

"Now we'll never get to meet the Alamo soldier who kept the Harrisburg flag," Sarah said, sadly. She had just heard Archie say that all Texans at the Alamo had been killed. "We can only hope that the little Lone Star gave him some comfort."

News of the Alamo swept Texas, leaving colonists angry about the defeat. A neighbor stopped on his way to Gonzales to join the army. He also reported on activities of the delegates at Washington-on-the-Brazos. "They selected David G. Burnet to serve as president of Texas until we have time for an election. Lorenzo de Zavala is vice-president."

Texans feared that Santa Anna would destroy all Texans, just as he had those at the Alamo, the neighbor said. Rumors said the Mexican army was marching across Texas. Other rumors reported that General Houston wanted Texans to cross the Sabine River into the United States territory. There they would be safe from the Mexican army.

The delegates at Washington believed the rumors. They moved the capital of Texas to Harrisburg, and many delegates prepared to move their families out of Texas.

The next day, Felix and Ernesto Moreno rode over to say a sad goodbye to the Dodsons. "We have loaded everything into our wagon," Felix said. "Today, we will go to Harrisburg to ask *Señor* Lorenzo de Zavala to guide us to safety."

"Sulema said to tell you we always will keep you in our thoughts," Ernesto said, trying to cover tears and the fright he felt. "Tell George I will miss him." Then the brothers rode quickly back home to their waiting family.

After the Morenos left, the Richardson family passed the Bradley cabin. They drove their wagon at a terrifying speed, frantically trying to get out of Texas.

By afternoon, Archie was in a panic over the welfare of Sarah. "I don't know what we should do," he said. "I can't tell which stories are true and which are rumors."

"If we are to go, the whole family needs to go together for safety," Sarah told him. "Let's pack what we can and go to Sandy Point before deciding about the trip."

They loaded the buggy and made their way to Sandy Point, arriving at Liza's cabin in a heavy rainstorm. They could see Chester and George busily getting the family ready to move toward the Sabine. Soon an anxious brother, Edward, arrived by horseback from Fort Bend County.

"General Houston told his men to burn Gonzales," Edward reported as he dismounted. "Then there will be nothing left to help the Mexican army. I hear that Houston's Texas army left Gonzales on March 12, moving eastward in retreat toward the Brazos. Houston is trying to stay between the Mexican army and those of us who are trying to get out of Texas. I believe all the rumors," Edward assured his mother. "We'd better get out of here fast and join this Runaway Scrape everybody is talking about.

"We need to move and move quickly," he said. "Yes, George, even before you ask, I'll agree that Wolf can go with us. Right now, I need both you and Wolf to help me drive the livestock down into the canebrakes along the river. Then, let's hide some furniture in the woods. We will dig a pit where we can bury the smaller items we can't take with us. Whatever is left will probably be burned by one of the armies."

Ignoring the continuing rains, Archie and Chester chose horses and firearms for the trip. Nancy made decisions about what would be loaded into the wagon. Sarah and her mother worked at melting lead and molding bullets.

Liza called the family together at her cabin that evening for Bible reading and prayers. Chester then explained the plan for the trip.

"Edward will ride ahead and tell us which road is best," he said. "That way, we won't waste time going the wrong way. The other men will help take care of the wagon and the buggy. Let's hope that the vehicles don't break down and that we all stay well. We can expect muddy roads and flooded rivers during the whole, miserable trip.

"We're planning to drive north to El Camino Real, then turn east toward Nacogdoches and Louisiana," he added. "We expect to meet John Bradley and the Tallys along the way."

The Bradleys, Gorbets, Dodsons, and old Callie left before daybreak the next day. They headed out along the same roads that had brought their families to Texas years earlier.

Bedding, cooking utensils, and food supplies filled the back of the ox wagon. Bradley men took turns driving it. The other men and boys rode horseback. When they weren't walking, women and girls rode in the wagon or in the horse-drawn buggy. Nancy insisted on taking the buggy, in hopes that Sarah and their mother could ride more comfortably.

Every day they passed cabins left empty, fields and barnyards utterly forgotten. They were reminded of how sad their own cabins looked when they left.

"It's a terrible thing to see all of Texas so overcome

by fear," Liza said sadly. Thunderstorms roared over them almost every day and night. On the slow journey along the muddy roads, Liza pointed to dishes and furniture smashed and scattered in the mud. She knew they were thrown away to lighten the weight of a bogged wagon.

During the day, Liza's family stopped only when the animals needed to rest. Of course, humans weren't allowed to be tired until after dark. On many days, they had no food except cold bread and jerky. Sometimes the rain kept them from building a fire for cooking. Other times, they didn't want to take time to cook.

At night, Edward selected the best place he could find for their camp. While the women made their beds in the wagon, the men set up tents in hopes of getting some rest from the drenching rains.

The frantic trip was hard for everyone, but the Bradleys thought mainly about Sarah and the baby expected in April. She said little and tried to be as cheerful as possible when the others came near her.

After starting the trip riding in the buggy, Sarah and her mother later moved to the wagon. It seemed more comfortable, even when rain came through openings in the wagon cover and dampened most of the bedding.

The men spent most of their time worrying about the crossing of every rain-swollen stream. Late one day, they neared the flooding Trinity River. Ahead of them, they could see a long line of wagons and carriages, whose drivers impatiently waited for the ferry. Many passengers suffered from measles or whooping cough.

"It will be days before we get our turn," Chester reported. He had ridden down to the river to ask about passage on the ferry. "What else can we do except wait?" he asked, discouraged for the first time his family could ever remember.

When she realized how her husband felt, Nancy somehow mustered up enough energy to try to boost spirits. "Gather round, everybody," she demanded, dragging her wet skirts through the mud to the back of the wagon. "We need a family conference, here and now!"

No one felt like moving, but they automatically followed Nancy's directions. When she had them in a circle around her, she began shouting as if she were angry with them.

"Look at yourselves!" she yelled. "You're the ugliest, wettest, muddiest, sorriest looking bunch I've ever seen!" She paused to scowl at them. "If you're my family, I want to know something." She paused again, then laughed and completed her statement. "Why aren't you smart enough to get in out of the rain?"

With that, she picked up a handful of mud and slung it at George and at her own children. She also hit just about everyone else. Soon, the other adults became aware of the teasing in her statements. They also realized they'd have to join the mud fight to protect themselves.

Within minutes, everyone was covered with mud. All were laughing as if they were having the happiest time of their lives. Wolf's fur was crusted with mud. He barked happily and ran with the children when they went to find more mud for throwing.

With the mud battle over, Nancy leaned against the wagon to rest. She looked up to see a somber-looking man passing by. She said solemnly, "Sir, I ask you, have you ever seen a worse looking bunch than this?"

The elderly rider stopped and looked around in alarm. He moved his gaze from face to muddy face. He finally asked, "Is that you, Liza Bradley? It's really hard to recognize anybody in this mud—I mean, rain."

Liza stepped forward to get a better view of him. "Yes, it's me, Rev. Fullenwider. It's wonderful to see you even in these terrible times when we don't know what is to become of us. As you can see, the young people were having some fun, just to relieve the weight of our problems."

"Yes, I see that they were," he replied, obviously in doubt that a mud fight would relieve anything. Then he looked at Sarah and back to Liza.

"I believe this is your daughter. My wife and I would like for you to bring her to our home. It's just down the hill near the ferry boat landing. You both can rest until the ferry is ready for your family."

Everyone felt relieved to see the preacher tie his horse to the back of the buggy. He then drove Sarah and Liza away. The two returned to the family wagon to make the difficult crossing of the Trinity.

Days later, near Nacogdoches, they camped close to the tents of two other families. Before going to bed, the adults visited briefly in one of the tents.

A man who had ridden horseback from San Felipe stopped in, also, and gave disturbing news to the others. "After the Alamo fell, James Fannin and his men were killed at Goliad," he told them. "I have heard that Santa Anna left San Antonio on March 31, moving this way. He has been burning cabins and barns wherever he went. I also was told that he ordered his soldiers to burn Brazoria."

Then the man turned to stories of the Texas army. "Sam Houston retreated from Gonzales, and he's still retreating. Right now, there is nothing left in San Felipe. For some reason, Houston's men decided to burn it. Somebody said they did it by mistake, but I don't know about that. I just know I rode through there later, and it had all burned to the ground."

The families from Sandy Point continued eastward as fast as possible. Early on April 9, 1836, they reached their goal, the Sabine River. Again they waited for a chance to cross the river by ferry.

For the first time on the whole trip, Sarah told her mother that she really did not feel well. Edward was notified. When they crossed the Sabine, he found a good camping place not far beyond the river. The family set up their tents and prepared to remain there as long as necessary. They were thankful to have arrived safely in Louisiana, away from the dangers of Santa Anna's army.

That evening, baby Maria was born, the first Dodson

child. A few days later, the wife of the ferry boat captain stopped by to see that Sarah and her daughter were both in good health. "As far as I know, this is the first Runaway Scrape baby born on the east side of the Sabine," she said.

With his wife and baby in a safe place, Archie wanted to go back to Texas. "I keep thinking about Sam Houston and the Texas army," he told Sarah. "It is time for me to join up again. I saw the Texans win in San Antonio. I just know we can win again."

This time Sarah didn't repeat the brave words she had spoken when he rode off to war with the Harrisburg troop. She didn't say anything, but quietly went on with the work around their tent.

It had been only a year since she and Archie married. In that one year, she sent her husband to war, lived through the Runaway Scrape, and gave birth to Maria. *These experiences have changed me a lot,* she thought to herself. *The only thing I want for my family now is to be together and safe.*

Without noticing that Sarah was unusually quiet, Archie spent the day getting ready to go back toward the Brazos. That was where he could find Houston's army, according to what he had heard in Nacogdoches. By afternoon, however, Archie had begun to feel sick. He went on with his work, but at suppertime he didn't want anything to eat. Callie said, jokingly, "Miss Sarah, I think this man must be sick! I've never known him to miss a chance to eat!"

Sarah felt his forehead and discovered that Archie was feverish. When Callie took a closer look at him, she knew what was wrong. "It's the measles," she said. "I know because I've had the measles myself, and I've seen plenty of other cases."

Archie was sent to bed in a tent away from the others. By morning, he was burning with fever. Callie decided she would take care of him and refused to allow Sarah and the baby to come near.

When Archie didn't recover quickly, members of Sarah's family also helped with his care. He hovered near death for several days before the fever finally broke. It was two weeks before he mended enough to leave his tent for a very long period.

Archie was asleep, still recovering from his illness, when the ferry boat captain came running up from the river with important news. "We finally won!" he shouted, when Chester went out to meet him. "Old Sam beat Santa Anna. Texas is free, at last!"

"Now, how did this happen?" Chester wanted to know. "Tell us more about it!"

"All I heard was that it took place at San Jacinto, on April 21," the man answered. "You might as well start packing to go back to Texas!" He hurried on his way to carry the good news to other Texans in tents nearby.

12

Rebuilding Texas

Late in May, Archie fully recovered from the measles, and family members learned for sure that the San Jacinto news was true. They joined many other families in crossing the Sabine, ready to begin a hard drive back to the Brazos.

On the way, they stopped again at the Fullenwider home. After holding baby Maria for only a moment, Mrs. Fullenwider tried to persuade the women and children to remain with her.

"Find out if your homes still stand before you take your womenfolk and children back to the Brazos," she said to the men. "I know that Archie expects to go back to the army soon. Sarah and the baby can stay right here until he finishes his army service and comes back for them."

Chester, Edward, and George, along with Wolf, knew that travel would be easier without the worry of a wagon and a buggy. Archie, still thin and pale from his illness, agreed with them but felt great sadness about leaving Sarah and Maria.

"You'll be so busy that the time will pass quickly for you," Sarah said to soothe him. "You know that we will be well cared for here, and you and I can try to get some mail through to each other."

"Having women along on a trip really does complicate things," George said to Liza and the other women before the four rode west. "Just one thing worries me, though. I know we won't eat very well until all of you get home to cook for us."

When the men arrived in the Brazos country, they stopped first at Sandy Point. As Edward had predicted, Liza's new cabin and all of Chester's buildings had been burned by Mexican soldiers. The soldiers also took what they could use from the fields.

"George, let's see if they found the valuables we buried," Edward said. "Help me find a shovel."

The men were looking through the charred remains of the barn when a neighbor stopped by to visit.

"While you're digging around here, you might look for a Mexican cannon," he suggested. "Mexican General Cos was near here when he heard that the Texans had won at San Jacinto. Everybody thinks he buried a cannon somewhere around here before he took his troops back to Mexico."

Unable to find a shovel, Archie and the others rode on to the Bradley place. They found everything exactly as they had left it. Archie's small crop of corn and other vegetables was still alive and growing, in spite of too much rain in March and April.

"This place must not have been in the army's path when they marched toward Harrisburg and San Jacinto," Edward said. "At least we'll have a good place to live while we rebuild Chester's property and round up the livestock along the river." He and George found a shovel and went back to dig up the buried items at Chester's place.

Several travelers who passed the Bradley home told Archie that almost everything had burned in Harrisburg. He took a few days from work on the Brazos to go there and see for himself. It was as he had heard. Nothing remained of the little house he had shared first with his father and then with Sarah.

"All we have from our Harrisburg home is that rocking chair," he thought, as he turned his horse away from

103

the torched village. "It's a good thing that I had that peddler take it back to Sarah at the Bradley house."

On June 26, Archie signed up for six months of duty in the Texas army. George promised to look after the small crop of vegetables until the Dodsons returned to the plantation. Before Archie left, Chester had returned to the Fullenwiders to load Nancy and her children into the wagon, bound for their new cabin at Sandy Point.

Nancy brought word that Sarah, baby Maria, and Liza planned to remain at the preacher's home in East Texas until Archie left the army. They were mourning the sudden death of Callie, who had spent so many years taking care of the Bradley family.

"Mrs. Fullenwider developed a great fondness for Maria," Sarah wrote in a note that Nancy delivered to Archie. "It will be better for us to remain here until you can come for us. Mama isn't yet ready to face the losses at Sandy Point without Callie."

Archie's army assignment placed him in Company A of the First Texas Regiment. At first he helped guard General Santa Anna and some of his men. The Mexicans were being held on a plantation a few miles down the Brazos River from the Bradleys.

"Everybody is very nervous around here," Archie wrote to Sarah. "President Burnet thinks we need to be prepared for another Mexican invasion to rescue Santa Anna at any moment."

Then Archie moved to an army camp at Dimitt's Landing on Lavaca Bay. At the end of only three months, when no Mexican invasion had come, Captain William S. Fisher signed Archie's furlough papers. Like many others, Archie was expected to spend the final three months of his army time at home, helping to rebuild Texas.

In late August, 1836, Archie notified Sarah that he was on his way to take her and the baby, along with Liza, back to the Brazos. Anxious to get home after six months in East Texas, Sarah asked Rev. Fullenwider to help her drive the buggy to meet Archie at the Trinity River.

104

When the family was reunited, Sarah and Archie needed time to make family plans. "You can see that all the hardships have taken their toll on Mama," Sarah said to Archie as they rode home from the Trinity. "I don't think she can live alone now. I hope that you and I, the baby and Mama, can live together at the old Bradley place. George has said he wants to work with Chester while saving his money to buy a steamboat for the Brazos River. I understand that he has moved his dog and his horse to Sandy Point."

Back at the old Bradley property, Archie worked on the place while Sarah set up a daily routine for her chores around the cabin. It was much like the work she did before she married, except that now she spent time looking after her husband and a baby, as well as Liza.

The Republic of Texas had promised Archie a land grant to help pay for his time in the Texas army. In his way of thinking, that land grant would replace the property lost in Harrisburg.

Early in January of 1837, while Sam Houston served as the president of the Republic, Archie rode over to the presidential office in the new town of Houston. He found lots of other former Texas soldiers waiting there in the office. Like Archie, they all were trying to get the land grants they had been promised.

Archie didn't get to talk to the president, and he learned nothing about his land grant. Instead, he rode home with sorrowful news for Sarah and Liza. Stephen Austin, the Father of Texas, had died December 27, 1836, at age forty-three.

"I remember when he came to see your papa in Kentucky, to tell us about Texas," Liza said, paying tribute to Stephen. "This fine gentleman led us to Texas, and he followed through on every promise he made us."

On a happier note, a new baby daughter joined the Dodsons in February 1838. Her name was Elizabeth, which was Liza's real name. About that time, the Bradley brothers in Fort Bend County asked Sarah and Archie to move closer to them. The Dodsons stayed in Fort Bend County several years, welcoming a baby son, Milton Dodson, in 1839.

Soon after Milton's birth, Archie decided to make a trip to the new Texas capital in Austin. He returned in a happy frame of mind because his land grant had been approved and because he brought exciting news for Sarah.

"I saw your flag, Sarah!" he told her as she and the two children greeted him at the front gate.

At first Sarah didn't know what he meant. She was so busy with her home and family that she had not thought about the little flag in several years.

"I saw the new flag of the Republic of Texas," Archie said again, with excitement in his voice. "It's so much like your flag that I think someone must have copied yours. I drew a sketch of it for you," he said, handing her a piece of paper. "You see the white star? It's set on a blue background, just like yours was. The only differences are that this official flag is larger than yours, and the red and white stripes are horizontal."

Sarah asked Archie to hold baby Milton while she studied the sketch. As was her way, she said very little except to thank Archie for the news.

"You're the amazin' woman who set them all to thinking about a Lone Star design," he said, trying to get her to show the same excitement he felt. "Just don't forget your part in making that flag!"

Enjoying his words and looking very pleased with everything, Sarah went into the cabin to tuck the sketch inside her special box of keepsakes.

After supper and after the children went to bed, Sarah brought the sketch out again for Liza to see. "I wonder what James Ferguson knows about the new flag," she said to Archie. "He probably had something to do with the fact that the new flag of the Republic of Texas looks so much like the Harrisburg flag. Or maybe Mr. De Zavala remembered seeing my flag."

Soon after that, the Dodsons went to a patriotic gathering in the nearby town of Richmond, in Fort Bend County. Sarah hoped that someone would bring a new Texas flag. Sure enough, she was excited to see a Lone Star flag, waving freely in the breeze. Its staff was positioned near the speaker's stand, where Sam Houston and other Texas heroes would be honored that day.

Everything about the patriotic gathering was a wonderful experience for Sarah and her family. Many Texas babies were being named in honor of General Houston that year, and the Dodsons hoped their next baby would be a son they could name Houston Dodson. When the baby born in 1841 turned out to be a daughter, however, no one was surprised about the choice of names for her: Harriet Houston Dodson.

While enjoying her growing family, Sarah was saddened by the deaths of several family members. Nancy died in 1839. Soon afterward, Liza also was laid to rest in the little cemetery at Sandy Point.

As she mourned these losses, Sarah learned that her brothers would like to buy her part of the Bradley property. She was willing to sell. Then she asked Archie to select his new land further north, a distance away from her first Texas home.

"Let's go where I can forget how much I miss Mama and Nancy and the others," she said. "I'd like a place just like we've always wanted, a place where we will have a church and a school very near to us. Mama always wanted a church and a school for her family, but Texas didn't have many churches and schools then. Now Texas is more settled, and I'd like those important places available for our children."

In 1844 the Dodsons found just the right property in Grimes County. They traveled northward more than a hundred miles to settle near a community known as Bedias. To make the move, Sarah and the four Dodson children rode in one wagon, while Archie drove a borrowed wagon, loaded with furniture. Of course, Sarah's favorite rocking chair was included with that furniture.

Their log house in Grimes County was larger than the old home. It had a second floor of finished lumber and chimney of brick, with kitchen and dining room in a separate building. A long porch across the front of the house seemed to invite the many close neighbors to stop for a visit.

A new picket fence protected Sarah's garden and yard from wild animals. Sarah thought of her mother and old Callie as she began to plant shrubs and flowers at her new home.

About the time they settled into their new cabin, another daughter was born and named Sarah Belvedier Crawford Dodson.

It was then that Archie made a trip to the county seat at Navasota. When he returned, he brought a wonderful gift for Sarah and their five children. "This is for you, Sarah, because you're an amazin' woman who somehow always manages to get what she thinks is best for her family."

It was a document stating that the Dodsons had donated land where a school would be built.

"School will go on during the week," Archie explained. "Then, on Sundays, I'm hoping that Rev. Fullenwider will move here to conduct church services. People of the community want to name it the Bethel Presbyterian Church."

Sarah immediately read the land deed and was happy to realize that daughters Maria and Elizabeth also wanted to read the document. Both girls had practiced reading the Bible enough that they could make out most of the words.

"I also learned some important news while I was in Navasota," Archie continued. "Texas now has become the twenty-eighth state of the United States. The Lone Star flag of the Republic of Texas has been declared the official flag of the State of Texas."

Ten-year-old Maria Dodson listened carefully to her

father's words. "Are you talking about the flag our mother made? I'm not sure I understand all you have said about flags."

"Let me give you more details," Archie said. He walked toward a strange, old wagon seat that was leaning against a nearby tree. Sarah smiled to see her blue-eyed husband gather his five children around him and begin to tell again his favorite story.

"One day in Harrisburg, so long ago that you weren't even born, your amazin' mother made a little Lone Star flag," he began. He pushed the old, slouch hat to the back of his head and began a very long version of the story. The youngest children soon fell asleep, but his words kept the oldest ones spellbound until Sarah called them in to supper.

Men of the community built the schoolhouse of logs, then covered them with boards. The building measured fifteen feet wide and thirty feet long. It had a split-log floor, a door at one end, and one glass window on a side wall. The men also made school furniture: chair and desk for the teacher and rough benches for students.

The school house was ready for students in the fall of 1847. The day before school opened, Archie and Sarah took their children to see the new structure. Walking down the lane toward the building, the Dodsons looked as if they were having their own little parade. Sarah led the group, carrying the youngest Dodson child, Thaddeus Constantine Dodson. Archie followed with little Sarah, namesake of her mother. Then came the four older children, in single file.

Last in line, Maria skipped along because she was too happy to walk. One cause of her happiness was that she carried a flag. It was her own creation, a homemade version of the Texas flag her father had described for her. She had trouble getting the five-pointed, white star to look right until her mother gave her a star pattern from the quilting box. Now everyone, even Milton, said it was a beautiful flag.

109

The second reason for her happiness was that now she finally could attend a real school. Maria moved her flag to the head of the line of children and led the younger Dodsons into the new building. All of them looked at every part of the school and even tried sitting on the benches. Then they joined their parents in front of the building.

"Isn't it amazin'!" they heard their mother exclaim as she admired the school house. She didn't talk often, and they all listened carefully when she did talk.

"Isn't it amazin' to have a building for a school and a church, right here next to our farm!" she said, astounded with the family's good fortune. "I think that bright little Lone Star on our flag has helped to inspire Texans to work for this and for all the freedom we have. I hope that Texans can have a Lone Star flag forever. Do you suppose that could happen?"

"Mama, you know that Papa says you're an amazin', surprisin' woman," Maria said, taking hold of her mother's hand. "If you want Texas to have freedom and a Lone Star flag forever, I know you'll see to it that all your children work to make it happen!"

Glossary

Bexar — A section of early Texas, containing a settlement known as San Antonio de Bexar. That settlement has become the city of San Antonio, in Bexar County.

comisario — An elected official, under Spanish or Mexican law, serving districts of around 500 persons in early Texas; similar to a present-day justice of the peace.

empresario — A land agent or contractor who worked with the Mexican government to get people to settle the vast, empty land in early Texas. Stephen F. Austin was one of the *empresarios*.

hog killin' time — Before people had refrigerators, they waited until cold weather to butcher hogs. The cold weather would keep the meat from spoiling until it could be treated with salt or other preservatives.

homespun — A plain cloth made of homespun yarn.

matchmaker — A person who tries to arrange a marriage for others.

retreat — To be forced back by an enemy.

Runaway Scrape — In spring of 1836, settlers fled from Texas for fear that Santa Anna's army would harm them. Many of them returned to their Texas homes after Sam Houston's army defeated Santa Anna at the Battle of San Jacinto, April 21, 1836.

siege — To use an army to encircle a fortified place, intending to take it.

symbol — Something that stands for another thing. Symbols of Texas include the Lone Star flag, the State Seal, the mockingbird, the bluebonnet, etc.

Texans — During the days of the Republic of Texas, settlers were usually called Texians or Texicans.

traitor — A person who helps an enemy and goes against friends or country.

Bibliography

Books:

Abernethy, Francis Edward, ed. *Texas Toys and Games.* Texas Folklore Society XLVIII. Dallas, TX: Southern Methodist University Press, 1989.

Barker, Eugene C. *The Life of Stephen F. Austin, Founder of Texas, 1793–1836.* Austin: University of Texas Press, 1926.

Brown, John Henry. *History of 1685 to 1892.* St. Louis, MO: L. E. Daniell, 1892.

Fehrenbach, T. R. *Lone Star: A History of Texas and the Texans.* New York: American Legacy Press, 1968.

Gilbert, Charles E., Jr. *Flags of Texas.* Gretna, LA: Pelican Publishing Co., 1989.

Holley, Mary Austin. *Texas.* Baltimore, MD: Armstrong & Plaskitt, 1833.

James, Marquis. *The Raven: A Biography of Sam Houston.* Garden City, NY: Blue Ribbon Books, 1929.

Jordan, Terry G. *Texas Log Buildings: A Folk Architecture.* Austin: University of Texas Press, 1978.

Muir, Andrew Forest, ed. *Texas in 1837.* Austin: University of Texas Press, 1958.

Newcomb, W. W., Jr. *The Indians of Texas, from Prehistoric to Modern Times.* Austin: University of Texas Press, 1961.

Pool, William C. *A Historical Atlas of Texas.* Austin, TX: Encino Press, 1975.

Rabb, Mary C. *Travels and Adventures in Texas in the 1820's.* Waco, TX: W. M. Morrison, 1962.

Smithwick, Noah. *Evolution of a State, or Recollections of Old Texas Days.* Austin, TX: Steck Co., n.d.

Turner, Martha Anne. *The Life and Times of Jane Long.* Waco, TX: Texian Press, 1869.

Webb, Walter Prescott, ed. *The Handbook of Texas.* Austin: Texas State Historical Association, 1952.

Articles:

Barneburg, Tina. "Creator of Texas Flag Finally Given Her Due." *San Antonio Express-News,* April 23, 1986.

Dobie, Dudley R. "A Son of the Texas Revolution." *Frontier Times* 9, no. 12 (September 1932), Bandera, TX.

Greenwood, J. H. "The Runaway Scrape." *Frontier Times* 4, no. 6 (March 1927), Bandera, TX.

Scott, Bess W. "Long May She Wave." *Texas Highways,* January 1984.

Tubbs, Edna May. "Sarah Bradley Dodson, 'Betsy Ross of Texas,' Is Honored." *San Antonio Express,* September 22, 1935.

Unpublished Sources:

Dodson family letters in Center for American History, University of Texas at Austin.

Stories from families of Sarah Bradley Dodson, William Tom, and George W. Smith.